THE SEA WATCH

A MYSTERY BY

BEVERLY KELLER

FOUR WINDS PRESS

NEW YORK

Grateful acknowledgment is made for the use of "With 'Er Head Tucked Underneath 'Er Arm" by R. P. Weston and Bert Lee. © 1934 Francis Day & Hunter Ltd. Reproduced by permission of EMI Music Publishing Ltd. 138-140 Charing Cross Road, London WC2H OLD, ENGLAND.

Library of Congress Cataloging in Publication Data

Keller, Beverly.
 The sea watch.
SUMMARY: While aboard a luxury liner bound for Europe, a young boy who is plagued by allergies stumbles onto a mystery involving a wristwatch.
 [1. Clocks and watches — Fiction. 2. Allergy — Fiction.
3. Mystery and detective stories] I. Title.
PZ7.K2813Se [Fic] 80-70000
ISBN 0-590-07703-1

Published by Four Winds Press
A division of Scholastic Inc., New York, N.Y.
Copyright © 1981 by Beverly Keller
All rights reserved
Printed in the United States of America
Library of Congress Catalog Card Number: 80-70000
1 2 3 4 5 85 84 83 82 81

To Cyrus, Gladys, and Ann

CONTENTS

CHAPTER ONE

EASTER

"I SAY HE'S PICKY." Fortney Potter's Grandmother Royce regarded him as she might a fish of dubious aroma. "I go to all this trouble making Easter dinner, and he picks at it."

"We go through this every holiday." Alice, Fortney's mother, spoke in the careful tone of one determined to be reasonable whatever the provocation. "You know he has allergies. Melons, nuts, and berries give him a rash. Meat and fish and fowl give him headaches. Besides, he's turned vegetarian."

"I think that's admirable." Elena, Alice's younger sister, smiled at Fortney.

He kept his eyes on the tablecloth, in the hope he might eventually be overlooked.

"Having headaches is admirable?" Grandfather Royce poured gravy into the crater in the center of his mashed potatoes.

"Being vegetarian is," Elena said.

"We do not talk religion at the table," Grandmother Royce decreed sternly. She returned to the study of Fortney. "I often wonder if the boy was intended for this planet. I mean, how can he be allergic to wool *and* cotton? We keep special sheets and blankets for his visits, and now he claims he's allergic to my beds. What is a person to think?"

"I would think he was allergic to your beds," Elena offered.

Grandmother Royce leveled a steely glance at her younger daughter.

"It's the mattress." Sugar cubes plinked into Alice's coffee like beads from a rosary of tribulations.

Grandfather Royce looked up. "What is?"

"What is what?" Alice asked.

"The matter."

"*Mattress*," Elena explained. "Fortney is allergic to your mattress."

"How does he know?" Grandfather Royce demanded.

Alice gripped her cup with both hands, as if it were the throat of some ravening beast. "He's been sneezing or wheezing or itching all his life. By now he knows exactly what's giving him trouble. At home, he sleeps on a foam matttress."

"Why not an egg carton?" Grandmother Royce sliced the key lime pie with swift savage precision.

All this might be useful some day, Fortney thought.

In a secret ceremony, the President pins a secret medal on the jacket of Fortney Potter, secret agent. "Masterful, Potter. Brilliant. Two years of dangerous assignments, and never caught."

Potter smiles thinly. "The secret, sir, lies in never being noticed."

"But, Potter, a man of your wit, accomplishment . . . style – how do you avoid notice?"

"Years of training, sir. Every Easter, I had dinner at my grandparents'."

After dinner, Fortney sat in a corner of the parlor leafing through old *National Geographic* magazines in search of horrifying pictures.

Grandmother Royce eyed him darkly. "If the boy would go out and play, he'd get over these allergy notions."

"Mother." Alice's voice sank ominously. "For twelve years I have been telling you. Grass and weeds and flowers make him sneeze."

Fortney sniffled.

Alice narrowed her eyes. "Has your cat been in here, Mother?"

"Not since you set foot in the house."

Alice's voice slid up an octave. "You know he can't be in a room a cat has even visited."

" . . . or a dog, bird, hamster, mouse. . . . " Grandmother Royce recited wearily. "We all have to live in this world, Alice, and the world is full of people with cotton shirts and wool sweaters and birds and beasts and pets."

Grandfather Royce eyed Fortney morosely. "Pets? The boy has never owned so much as a goldfish."

"If it leaped out of its bowl, he'd have a real headache," Alice said. "They do, you know."

"Who?" Grandmother Royce asked.

"Goldfish. Leap out of their bowls." Alice turned to Elena. "Ours always did when we were little, remember? They do it from spite."

"Boredom, more likely," Elena ventured.

"If he were mine," Grandfather Royce declared, "I'd send him to military school, or camp. Make a man of him."

Fortney had a wavering vision of a goldfish in khaki uniform staggering under a tiny backpack, feathery gills merging into a hint of beard. . . .

"He is allergic to horses." Fortney's father spoke like a man who has become almost resigned to a deadening burden. "And you can't find a camp away from grass or weeds."

"Or a military school with foam beds and special sheets," Grandmother Royce added innocently.

Elena leaned over the back of her chair. "Fortney, how would you like to spend a month in Paris, with nylon sheets and foam pillows? Charles and I are sailing June eighth for France."

"Send my only son to sea?" Alice stared at her in astonishment. "What a marvelous idea."

"Alice!" Fortney's father admonished.

She recalled herself almost at once. "I mean, the ocean is free of weeds, grass, horses. . . ."

"No — Charles and I planned the ocean trip as a second honeymoon," Elena said. "We thought Fortney could fly over later to join us."

"Second honeymoon." Grandmother Royce smiled tolerantly. "Elena, Elena — you belong to another age."

Elena, Fortney mused, belonged in an age when women wore swirling peach-colored silk and long capes that smelled of heather — however heather smelled. Tall and slender, with a low furry voice, hair as soft and gold as a collie pup, and eyes the color of cider, she'd been married two years to Charles D'Aubigne, a French diplomat stationed in Washington. When Grandmother Royce mentioned Charles to acquaintances, which she did at every opportunity, she promoted him to "a French ambassador." Privately, she confided to relatives, "With all the fine young American men after her, I don't know why Elena had to pick somebody with an apostrophe in his name."

Elena stood now. "I must go. Let me know about Paris, Fortney."

At the door, Grandmother Royce kissed her. "Give our love to Charles. I'm sorry he didn't come with you. Of course, being French, he probably looks down on good old-fashioned American family gatherings."

Bending to hug Fortney, Elena murmured, "Being French, Charles has an instinct for self-preservation."

When she had gone, Fortney's father turned to him.

"Son, I hope you realize what a fantastic opportunity this is."

And Fortney understood the choice — go to Paris, or hear for the rest of his life what an opportunity he'd missed.

He spent the next weeks sick to his stomach, trying to decide whether he wanted to go. Meanwhile, his parents got him a passport and new clothes.

#

CHAPTER TWO

JUNE FIRST

ON JUNE FIRST, Elena telephoned from Washington. "Fortney, how would you like to meet me in New York in a week and sail to France?"

"Elena!" Alice cried over the extension in her room. "You've left Charles!"

"No, no," Elena assured her, "but he can't get away from Washington before July. It's too late to cancel our ship passage and get a refund. Forfeiting that money and then paying for Fortney to come over later would be silly."

"I don't have all my clothes yet, and I need special bedding," he protested.

"I can arrange bedding," she said, "and we can buy what you need in Paris."

When the call was over, he burst into his mother's room. "I can't get ready in a week! School isn't over until June sixth."

"What do you have to do? I've done all the shopping and running around for you."

"I have to prepare my mind."

His mother rested her hands on his shoulders.

"Fortney, think of it. It's the fastest, newest, most revolutionary ship in the world. Not a smidgen of dust. No pets. No pollen, no allergies, no shots."

He could not remember a day he'd not itched or sneezed or wheezed. For six years he'd gotten allergy shots every Monday and Friday.

His stomach heaved like a beached jellyfish. But in some mysterious part of his mind he realized that if he left in a week, he wouldn't have to worry for a whole month about whether or not he wanted to go.

CHAPTER THREE

ON BOARD

SO FORTNEY POTTER, his mind all unprepared, flew to New York on June eighth and boarded the fastest ocean liner ever built.

"A miracle," Charles D'Aubigne told him. "A revolution in shipbuilding — New York to Southampton in four days. With the price of oil soaring, this was inevitable. What else can carry more than a thousand people at a trip, and with comfort, luxury? After decades of being crammed like herring aboard aircraft, travelers are starved for a civilized carrier."

"Is Southampton in France?" Fortney asked dubiously.

"No, no. England. Ships used to sail first to Cherbourg — *that's* France — then to Southampton, but this one docks first at Southampton, then goes on to Cherbourg. I'm sure there's a reason." He handed Fortney a plastic card. "Do you know what this is?"

"A plastic card," Fortney said.

"On it is a magnetic code that unlocks the door of this suite, and no other. This one is for you." He looked at

Elena. "I would have filled this suite with flowers, but for his allergies."

"It was thoughtful of you not to." She touched Charles's cheek. "Besides, you spent far too much on my watch."

He kissed the wrist on which she wore the tiny jeweled timepiece. "My darling, after giving you three watches, I regret none of them."

While Charles kissed Elena's ears and neck and eyelids, Fortney kept his eyes resolutely on the New York skyline and wondered how anything ever got done at the French Embassy.

At the third announcement of "All visitors ashore, please," Charles led Elena and Fortney to the promenade deck. He said something bracing and hearty to Fortney. It was lost in the music from the orchestra at the bow. Charles kissed Elena so long Fortney was afraid there would be three of them sailing to Southampton; then he ran. It was a memorable exit.

As Fortney stood at the rail watching the crowds on shore wave and throw streamers, a ribbon of water widened between ship and dock.

"There's Charles," Elena said.

"Where?"

"He must be there somewhere by now." She leaned forward, waving. "Oh, lord! There goes my watch."

They struggled through the crowd and down a staircase to the deck below. Elena looked up. "We were standing about there, so it should have landed near here. As soon as people start going in we can see what was underfoot."

"I wonder what time it is," Fortney murmured. "I'm supposed to take my asthma pill at six."

"It's six-forty-five," a man behind Elena volunteered. Dark-haired, tall, tanned, he looked the way race-car drivers do in films, lean and dangerous and secretly amused.

"Thank you," Fortney said.

"I'll watch for my watch while you take your pill," Elena told Fortney.

Outside their suite, he held his card against the door, then turned the knob easily. Inside, he unpacked his prescription bottles, wondered where to array them, then put them back in his suitcase. After swallowing his asthma pill, he stepped into the corridor and unlocked the door with the card a few more times.

The man who'd told him the time came out of the door next to theirs.

"So you're in the Imperial Suite. That makes us neighbors." The man offered his hand. "Gerard Marais."

Fortney put the card in his pocket and shook hands firmly. "Fortney Potter. Just . . . checking out our door."

As they walked toward the elevator, Marais asked, "Is the woman with you your sister?"

"My aunt."

"She's very beautiful. Where will you sit at meals?

Why don't I arrange for us to share a table?"

Fortney wondered whether it would be appropriate to look faintly amused, or, possibly, faintly dangerously amused.

"She's married," he said.

"Look," Marais confided, "I should be delighted to learn she is not happily married. If she is, I shall admire her silently and discreetly. I'll meet you outside the dining room at eight."

Fortney found his aunt on deck, getting to her feet. She brushed her knees and showed him the remains of her watch.

He looked sympathetic. "Lucky you have two more."

"But I don't have them. I dropped one in the Cuisinart and wore the other skin-diving."

He took a sheaf of papers from his pocket. "I was supposed to give you these the minute I saw you. From Mother."

She read them walking to the elevator. He could see how she'd be hard on watches.

" 'No nuts, melon, berries, fish, fowl, meat' — you'll be a challenging dinner companion." She walked into a monstrous fern, murmured "Sorry," and went on reading. " 'No cotton, wool, feathers' — I've arranged for bedding, and I won't wear wool or cotton. What do you use for bath towels?"

"I drip dry. Cotton really doesn't bother me too much if I take my pills on time. That's the next page."

"Let me finish this one. 'No dogs, cats, rodents,

birds, horses, grass, trees, weeds, grasses.' . . . How fortunate we didn't sail by ark."

In the elevator, she read the second page. " 'Blue pills every two hours, pink every four, white every six, green every eight. Two whiffs from your inhaler if all else fails.' I hope you have a watch, Fortney."

"I did, but the band broke."

"We can do without the band."

"The watch got run over when the band broke. All the other papers are prescriptions in case I run out of anything."

She shoved them all in her purse. "It must be close to eight. The only things with which this ship is not lavishly equipped are clocks — I think we're supposed to sustain a mood of carefree, timeless abandon. At any rate, we don't change for dinner the first night out."

Fortney entertained the brief image of tables surrounded by passengers whose hands and faces were becoming hairy, canine teeth elongating. . . .

Outside the dining room, Gerard Marais introduced himself to Elena. "I've met your nephew. It seems we've been assigned the same table."

Fortney looked faintly amused.

The others at their table were reasonably interesting, for adults. A blond, blue-eyed man in a navy-blue uniform stood. "I'm Michael Baird, your purser." He looked to Fortney like a lifeguard, or a storm trooper out of some old war movie. The other man, Darius Heurtebise, introduced himself as if his own name were a source of great weariness to him. His eyes, brown and unspeakably disillusioned, rested on dark pouches. Strands of straight, sparse brown hair were combed sideways to cover the bare top of his head.

As Marais pulled out a chair for Elena, she looked at the roses and camellias in the center of the table. "I'm so sorry — my nephew is allergic to flowers."

"No problem." Like a knight who has dispatched a minor dragon, Baird bore away the offending blooms.

With the purser gone, Marais sat on Elena's right, Fortney between him and Heurtebise.

"What does a purser do?" Fortney asked Marais.

"He's the ship's officer responsible for keeping all the passengers happy."

An old woman stopped at their table. Her wiry gray hair sent tendrils in all directions, like a curious sea urchin. Her face had surrendered to time and gravity, so that she resembled an aged but amiable bloodhound.

She fixed her gaze on Heurtebise, who stood, along with Fortney and Marais. "So, Inspector. I have dreamed of meeting you some day." She turned to Fortney. "Inspector Heurtebise is a French national treasure like England's Sherlock Holmes, but, as you see, entirely real."

It was obvious that Heurtebise had never dreamed of meeting her. He pulled out the chair on his right and when she had seated herself he moved the chair toward the table rather as if he were closing a bureau drawer.

Marais sat again, rather quickly.

"I'm Gertrude Satchel," the old woman said.

Fascinated by her, Fortney was distracted by Marais, who shoved something up his sleeve.

Ms. Satchel seemed to have deepened the inspector's melancholy. "Please. I do not wish to be recognized. I do not wish to be asked my opinion of crime or punishment or what happened to someone's shoes which were set out to be polished. . . ."

"Ah, you are undercover!" Her voice sank to a conspiratorial growl. "How exciting."

He looked even more pained. "Not undercover, madame. Simply overtired."

She was not daunted. "You are traveling incognito, then?"

"Merely in privacy . . . if you will cooperate in keeping my identity undisclosed."

"Of course," she assured him.

"So far as any of us here are concerned, you are simply Mr. Heurtebise," Elena added.

"Have you been on vacation in America, Mr. Heurtebise?" Marais asked.

"One does not vacation in America." The inspector spoke with the flat certainty of one announcing an unchallengeable truth. "America is a jungle, a volcano, a Jacuzzi of the spirit."

Ms. Satchel hastened to rescue the conversation from Marais' faltered grasp. "Would it be impertinent, just between us, Inspector, to ask if you are working on a case?"

"I am all but retired from the war on crime," he said. "Crime has declined."

She seemed surprised. "Really? I thought there was more than there used to be."

"I am speaking of the quality of crime, madame, not the quantity. There is no elegance, no imagination, no style in crime today. Look at your television programs. *Bang Bang! Rob! Shoot! Kill!* Consider your cinema detectives. Animals. Brutes. Chase cars. Break cars. It is enough to have given me an ulcer, madame. The state of crime is a crime."

"What a shame," she murmured.

"Indeed. I have had to give up wine, spices, rage. . . ."

"And what brought you to America, then?" Marais persisted.

"My ulcer. I had heard of an American doctor who developed a new treatment. It did me no good. My wallet was stolen in her waiting room."

Baird returned to the table.

Elena smiled at him. "Thank you."

"Anything. Anytime." The purser looked as if he might kiss her hand at the slightest excuse.

While Fortney considered whether to look dangerous or slightly amused, Marais leaned toward her. "How far are you sailing?"

"Cherbourg. You?"

"Only to Southampton, which I now regret."

"Are you on vacation?" Baird asked him.

"Business," Marais said.

"What business are you in?" Baird asked.

"I'm with an American export-import firm."

His potato soup thickening, his poached egg staring up at him unnoticed, Heurtebise continued to enlighten Ms. Satchel on the state of crime.

Fascinated and more than a little intimidated, Fortney bit into a muffin. His teeth met in the grainy fullness of a pecan just as Heurtebise turned a brooding gaze on him.

Caught in that formidable glare, Fortney could not help but swallow.

"What is crime today?" Heurtebise demanded. "The mindless violence of overage delinquents. Except, of course, for underage delinquents; boys like this who run wild, terrorize the society which pampers them."

The itch began between Fortney's shoulder blades.

"All boys are barbarians," the inspector was saying. "Deranged. Savages from the cradle. Ah — you blush, boy."

"No . . . no, sir."

"Do not contradict me. Being a boy, you are a seething fen of criminal impulses. You blush because you know I speak the truth."

Fortney shook his head. "Nuts," he explained.

"NUTS?" The inspector's brush of moustache quivered. "*Nuts!* How dare you attempt to insult me with your vulgar American slang! I am an expert on American slang. I read American novels. I watch American films. I am appalled by their crudeness, but I have learned all the American slang. Do not scratch yourself at the table! What are you, boy, an ape?"

"Rash," Fortney muttered miserably.

The inspector's voice was frigid. "Rash, indeed. Rash and reckless."

Ms. Satchel leaned across him to peer at Fortney. "Why, the boy's all blotchy." She dipped her napkin in her water glass and passed the dripping cloth over the inspector's vanilla custard. "Cool your forehead, dear."

"Fortney, are you all right?" Elena came around the table and pressed the icy napkin to his brow. "Is it allergies?"

"Allergies?" The inspector's moustache vibrated in derision.

"Allergies, like ulcers, can be aggravated by certain foods," Ms. Satchel observed.

"Like ulcers?" His moustache stiffened with indignation. "Madame, one can see an ulcer. One can take an X-ray picture of an ulcer. Have you ever seen an allergy? Has anyone photographed an allergy?"

"May I be excused?" Fortney asked, desperate for a pill.

"I'll come with you," Elena offered.

"No, please." It was enough to cross the dining room

itching, wet, and flushed, without being escorted by his aunt.

She patted him reassuringly and returned to her seat, flicking Heurtebise with a gaze as chill as the water trickling under Fortney's collar.

The sofa in the sitting room of the Imperial Suite had been transformed into a bed, with blue silk sheets turned down over shimmery blankets.

After he took his pills, Fortney opened the draperies and stood before the window. He couldn't make out just where the moon-dappled sea met the night sky, but he realized suddenly what a vastness engulfed the ship. He felt solemn, almost forgetting how he itched.

He was still at the window, wondering if they were well north of the Bermuda Triangle, when Elena came in with Marais. "Michael Baird said we shouldn't miss the First Night Follies in the Empress Lounge, so Gerard and I came to fetch you. We'll see if Ms. Satchel wants to join us."

As they walked toward the elevator, Marais murmured, "If there were no others aboard, you'd notice how still and strange the night ocean is. You would also find yourself on an enormous ghost ship. I remember an English song my mother used to sing:

> In the Tower of London, large as life,
> The ghost of Anne Boleyn walks, I declare. . . .

He ushered Elena and Fortney into the elevator, then went on in a sort of Cockney accent:

> With 'er head tooked underneath 'er arm,
> She walks the bloody Tower,
> With 'er head tooked underneath 'er arm,
> At the midnight houuur. . . .

"*Tooked?*" Fortney whispered to Elena.

"That's *tucked* with a Cockney accent," she murmured back.

As they stepped out of the elevator into a long, deserted corridor, she confided, "If I ever meet a ghost, I hope I have the presence of mind to say something decent. It must be such a lonely life . . . nonlife . . . afterlife. Ah! There she is!"

Fortney's gulp of air escaped in a long whistling wheeze. Ahead of them, a man hurried away from a wraithlike figure in a long, swirling, gray robe.

Elena approached that gray apparition. "Ms. Satchel, will you come to the Follies with us?"

"Did you see that?" Ms. Satchel gazed after the departing man.

"Only his back," Elena said.

"I was putting my shoes out to be polished when he came out of the cabin across the hall. I said, 'You must be Mr. Arnold,' and he simply turned and fled. I'm not all that alarming."

"How did you know his name?" Fortney quavered.

"As soon as I board a ship I read the passenger list. Always hoping to find someone exciting from my past. Never have."

A door across the hall opened and Heurtebise emerged. As he bent to set his shoes down, Ms. Satchel said, "You should put them on and go to the First Night Follies."

He looked up at her. "Why?"

"To get your mind off things. Well, I'm for bed. Good night." She withdrew, shutting her door.

"There will be food at the Follies." Steadying himself against his door jamb, Heurtebise struggled into his shoes. "An ulcer requires frequent, depressing meals. Come."

••• FIRST NIGHT FOLLIES •••

The Empress Lounge was an enormous salon full of mirrors, gold trim, voices, and music.

The purser had saved a table for them. Standing to greet them, he beckoned a waiter. "Champagne, and a lemonade."

Heurtebise shook his head wearily. "No. I will have mineral water only."

"Good idea," Marais said. "Keeps the mind clear. I'll have the same." Reaching for Elena's hand, he guided her to the dance floor.

Ignoring the streamers and confetti falling around

him, Heurtebise gazed at the revelers. "What hope is there for a species which would wear paper hats and blow horns at one another in the name of pleasure? And who are those excessively muscular young men at the next table?"

Baird glanced briefly at that table. "Mountain climbers. American. You really should help yourselves at the buffet table before everything's covered with confetti."

The inspector stood. "Come, boy. If you do not eat properly, you may remain stunted forever."

In the inspector's wake, Fortney threaded among dancers, balloons, and noisemakers and circled the long buffet table.

Heurtebise gazed bleakly at the blond, bronzed mountain climber across from them piling pickled onions and tiny red peppers on a plate. "Torment. Torment." Heurtebise groaned. "From all this epicurean assemblage I may have only the most bland, banal, and boring. This, boy, *this* is my reward for dedicating myself to the preservation of law, of civilization itself — my twilight years spent among custards and cream cheese."

They returned to their table just as Elena and Marais finished dancing. Standing, Baird handed each of them a glass. "Mrs. D'Aubigne, Mr. Heurtebise, Marais — and, Fortney, your lemonade. May I propose a toast?"

A waiter touched his arm and whispered something in his ear.

Suddenly grim, Baird set down his glass. "I'm afraid

something has come up. Mr. Heurtebise, please continue with the toast." He hurried after the waiter.

The inspector's voice was tense but low. "Monsieur Marais, take care of the boy and his aunt. Someone must look after the other passengers. . . . Madame, it is one thing to be brave, another to be frivolous. This is no time to smile."

"But it is," Elena murmured. "The waiter whispered — I shouldn't tell."

"Madame!" the inspector sputtered.

She compressed her lips briefly, then said, "The floor show is about to start, but the ventriloquist's dummy has insulted the comedian, who is trying to strangle him."

"Attempted homicide is not amusing, madame. I will be needed." He pushed back his chair, jostling a mountain climber returning from the buffet table.

"It's the dummy that's being strangled," Elena said.

A cheese swirl slid off the mountain climber's plate into the inspector's glass.

Heurtebise gazed at the dissolving blob. "Let us hope the man is more sure-footed at the peak of Everest."

"Here." Marais offered his own glass to the inspector. "I haven't touched my drink. I want to get something to eat." He went with Elena to the buffet table.

Heurtebise summoned a waiter and handed him the water with the cheese drifting like minuscule showers

of confetti to the bottom. "Please remove this . . .
mixture and bring Monsieur Marais another mineral
water."

Sipping from the glass Marais had given him, Heurtebise gazed at the crowd like a Puritan observing a
pagan sacrifice.

Fortney wondered how far the comedian had gotten
in his dummycide. Would the floor show go on anyway?
Would the wooden head hang at some hideous angle?
Might it even be *tooked* under a small carved arm?

Elena and Marais returned to the table. Marais drank
his new mineral water without proposing a toast.
Fortney was relieved. Even looking faintly amused
would not lessen the awkwardness of drinking a toast in
lemonade.

Every few minutes, the mountain climbers exploded
in laughter. Heurtebise ignored them with the ice calm
of a nobleman.

Looking spent, the purser returned.

"What a shame," Elena told him. "We've finished
our drinks and you've not even touched yours."

"It doesn't matter," he said. "I don't think you'll want
to stay. There's been a problem with the floor show. We
should have it pulled together for tomorrow night's
Poseidon Party. Actually, it's always a good idea to get
to bed early the first night out. Jet lag and all that."

"Jet lag?" Elena repeated.

"Tidal fatigue . . . whatever."

Fortney leaned toward Elena. "I don't think I want to
see . . . anything . . . that's all pulled apart."

To his relief, she stood.

In the suite, she said, "Sleep well," and went into the bedroom and shut the door.

He slid between the cool sheets of his sofa bed, wondering how she could be so offhand after songs about headless ghosts and the talk of strangled dummies.

He woke in the dark.

The sounds came from the next suite — Marais'.

Fortney felt under his pillow for his inhaler. If someone . . . something . . . were crashing around Marais' suite with her . . . its . . . head *tooked* underneath an arm, what good would a twelve-year-old with allergies be?

Maybe Marais was unpacking, or jogging, or practicing karate.

But suppose the ship was on fire, or hijacked by a berserk comedian, or gripped by a Sargasso Sea?

Padding across the dark room, Fortney peered into the corridor.

There was a crash. Marais' door burst open. A stranger dashed out and raced past Fortney, dropping a wristwatch.

Then Marais, in pajama bottoms and hairy chest, staggered into the corridor holding his throat.

"Was that the comedian?" Fortney gasped.

Marais slumped against the wall.

"Should I get a doctor or somebody?"

"No! No. I'm all right."

Wavy kneed, but knowing something helpful was required, Fortney picked up the watch. "Well. At least you didn't lose this." As he held it out, he saw that Marais wore its twin on his wrist. "No — it's exactly *like* yours!"

Marais seized the watch and backed into his own suite.

As Fortney stared at the closing door, he felt a hand on his shoulder. "I heard voices. What are you doing out here?"

He turned, ashamed of the yip that had escaped him. "Elena, I think somebody tried to choke Mr. Marais."

She started banging on Marais' door. "Gerard?"

In curlers and confusion, passengers were peering out into the corridor.

Marais, in a wine-colored silk robe, opened his door. "Elena! What is it?"

"Are you all right?"

"Of course."

"That man who ran out of your suite. . . ." Fortney prompted.

"I'm afraid you've had a nightmare." Marais put his hand on Fortney's shoulder. Where a watch had been moments earlier, Fortney saw only a strip of skin paler than the rest of his arm.

"It's my fault," Marais said. "I shouldn't have been filling your head with songs about ghosts."

Baffled, embarrassed by the stares of the wakened

passengers, Fortney let his aunt draw him back into their suite.

"Elena, a man ran out his door."

She touched his cheek. "It was only a dream."

"It was not."

"Shall I sit up with you a while?"

"Not unless you're going to believe me."

"I'm not at my brightest at three in the morning, Fortney. Do you want your light out?"

When he didn't answer, she turned it out and left him alone with the darkness.

CHAPTER FOUR

THE SECOND DAY

•••MORNING•••

Fortney sat up. "I did not have a nightmare. There was a man."

Elena came out of the bedroom. "I admire your tenacity, but it's time to get ready for breakfast."

"I can tell you're not going to take this seriously."

She looked down at him. "All right. What do you want me to do? Shall I go to the captain? Shall I tell Gerard he was attacked by a mysterious assailant whether he thinks so or not? Shall I have the ship searched or someone flown out from Scotland Yard?"

He stalked into his bathroom.

Heurtebise, Ms. Satchel, and Marais were at their table when he trudged into the dining room yards behind his aunt. He sat next to Ms. Satchel.

She peered at him. "Did you get enough sleep? You look pale."

"Conscience," Heurtebise asserted. "The rare boy who has a conscience has a guilty one."

"And how did you sleep?" Ms. Satchel asked Heurtebise.

"Horribly."

Her face was impassive. "Oh?"

"Like a rock, a stick, as if I'd been drugged." He took a grudging bite of toast.

"I was drugged once," she volunteered.

"Madame!" Crumbs cascaded down his chin.

"I had tracked a rather infamous criminal to the Casbah, hoping to interview him for my newspaper. He was charming, but not at all trustworthy. Drugged by arak."

"Who was Eric?" Fortney asked, spellbound.

"Not Eric, arak," she said. "It's a potent liquor made from dates. When I awoke I was in the desert, where I was saved by a chivalrous sheik. Which was fortunate, because I would never have gotten far with my toes." She beamed at the approaching waiter. "Ah, scones. It's been ages since I had a decent scone for breakfast."

It was plain from the silence that everyone wanted to ask about her toes, but no one knew how to bring them back into the conversation. After a few moments, the talk meandered into random pleasantries.

When breakfast was over, Marais asked, "Elena, you'll join me for shuffleboard?"

"I have to finish unpacking."

"Do you play table tennis?" Marais asked Heurtebise.

"Tables," the inspector said firmly, "were meant for food."

"A stroll?" Marais asked Ms. Satchel.

"Exercise before noon," she declared, "is responsible for the decline of all advanced civilizations."

Marais smiled at Fortney. "How about a game of billiards?"

"I think I'm due to take a pill. What time is it?"

"I don't own a watch." Marais held Fortney's gaze a moment, then asked Ms. Satchel, "Shall we sit on deck?"

She hesitated. "Sounds bracing, but a bit chilly."

"I'll fetch your wrap," he offered.

She rummaged through an enormous lumpy tote bag and hauled out a card. "Cabin ten-forty. There's a gray sweater on the tan chair."

"That was foolish of you," Heurtebise told her when Marais left.

She seemed undisturbed. "You think that charming young man, who has a suite on the signal deck, would find anything in my cabin worth taking?"

"I am speaking on principle. Charming people make brilliant criminals."

Fortney spent the morning wandering through the ship, exploring deck after deck . . . theaters, shops, ballrooms, gymnasiums. The mountain climbers were in the Lobelia Lounge, poring over a map they'd spread on the table before them, talking about *pitons*, *glissades*, and *moraines*. Fortney sat close enough to overhear without actually eavesdropping. The blond climber from the night before, a man the others called Kurt, glanced at him. Fortney left the lounge, trying to look faintly amused.

••• AFTERNOON •••

"This ship is like a city, only stacked in layers," Fortney told Ms. Satchel at lunch.

She nodded. "Something like Katmandu."

"Cat men do what?"

"Kat-man-du," she repeated carefully. "The capital of Nepal. I can still see it as I first came upon it — the dry clean air and that fantasy of a city. I was riding yak-back after weeks of climbing the Himalayas. This was before my toes, of course. And here I am, not much over seventy, settling for speaking engagements in London. It's because of my children. They were un-done when I overstayed my visit with New Guinean headhunters. Children tend to go stodgy at forty."

"Stodgy people," Heurtebise put in, "make the most meticulous criminals."

"Speaking of stodgy," she said to Fortney, "you re-member Mr. Arnold, who fled me first night out? I haven't seen him since. Not at meals, not on deck, nowhere. I hope the poor soul isn't lying seasick in his cabin."

"I might envy him." Heurtebise gazed at his cream of celery soup.

After lunch, Elena and Marais walked around the promenade deck. Fortney wondered if he owed it to Charles to accompany them. He decided not. Elena would never be untrue with a man who lied about watches.

He settled himself on the deck chair next to Ms. Satchel's. "Real headhunters?"

"Oh, yes."

"Weren't you scared?"

"My head was never that ornamental."

"What were you doing in the Himalayas that other time?"

"Looking for the Lama."

"That's like a small camel?"

"*Llama* with two *l*s is like a small camel. *Lama* with one *l* is a holy man. I was on my way to Tibet. At that time it was a mystical place."

"Mythical?"

"Mystical. Mystical is out of the ordinary, but real. Of course, there are mythical things which may be real. Dragons, for instance. One nearly did me in on Komodo."

"You mean like a Japanese bathrobe?"

"Komodo is an island. This was a Komodo dragon."

He sat up straighter. "There really are dragons?"

"Of course. Komodos run about ten feet long, and fast, especially when pursuing people. Your Loch Ness Monster, on the other hand, is a peaceful beast. Otherwise, he'd surely have harmed the humans who've harassed his haunts for generations. Wouldn't you say?"

"There is a Loch Ness Monster?"

"I hope so. When there's a difference of opinion on any subject, I choose to believe the more interesting. Fortney, you must do something about that wheeze."

He didn't want to say it was because of her cotton dress. "It must be time for my pill."

He climbed the stairs to the Imperial Suite. . . . *Suntanned, excessively muscular, Fort Potter struggled to the summit of the forbidden peak, where he planted his country's flag.* . . . And took his pill.

••• LATER THAT DAY •••

Ms. Satchel was not where he'd left her. He wandered the ship, stalking past the children's play area, finally venturing into a sauna where he lay sweating, hiding in a Himalayan jungle, pursued by headhunters and dragons.

When he trudged into the dining room at eight, Elena nodded at him. He was glad to see Baird, the purser, at her right. Marais would have to work for her attention.

"You will come to the Poseidon Party tonight," Baird urged her. "I promise it will be better than the First Night Follies."

"We may give it a try," Marais said.

"Would you like to go, Fortney?" Elena asked.

"There's a Christopher Lee movie at the theater tonight."

"I'm not sure you should see it," Elena said. "You didn't sleep well."

"Conscience," Heurtebise pronounced.

Elena snapped a bread stick. "His conscience, Mr. Heurtebise, is no concern of yours."

"And you would permit him to fill his brain with terror films? At your age, boy, you should be reading the classics."

"At his age, he is quite capable of deciding for himself."

"So am I going?" Fortney asked.

"Of course," Elena said, glaring at the inspector.

"Would you mind terribly if I came with you?" Ms. Satchel asked Fortney. "I can't resist a mystery. I have one myself, by the way."

"A conscience?" Heurtebise inquired.

"A mystery. Have you ever taken apart a tape recorder, Fortney?"

"When I was six. I got sent to my room for it."

"The most extraordinary thing happened just before dinner," she said. "I tried to tape my notes for my Explorer's Club lecture, but the machine balked. I took it apart, and look what was stuffed among its innards." She fished a silver-colored wristwatch from her purse.

"It's exactly like your two!" Fortney told Marais.

The response was cool and clear. "I have no watch, but you seem to have an obsession with them, Fortney. And they all look alike, do they? A psychiatrist might find that intriguing."

"That's enough, Gerard," Elena said sharply.

"I would suspect, Ms. Satchel, that some workman at the recorder factory is still wondering where his timepiece went." Marais sounded amused.

"American workmanship," Heurtebise observed.

"Fortney," Ms. Satchel said, "would you do me a favor? Would you put the watch in my cabin so it doesn't bang around in my purse? The band is too big for my wrist. Then, if you'd bring me the glasses from my bedside table, I'll be able to see the film." She handed him the watch and her door card.

"You can't leave valuables around!" Marais protested.

"I would hardly call that a valuable watch. Shall I meet you at the theater, Fortney?"

As he stood, Elena reminded him, "You'd better take your pills before the movie."

He nodded, and hurried away.

In the elevator, he slipped the watch over his sleeve, holding his arm up like a surgeon who has scrubbed. Despite his embarrassment and his rage at Marais, he was baffled and fascinated by the mystery — three watches, identical, appearing, disappearing.

When he turned on the bathroom faucet, the watch slid down to his knuckles. He put it on the shelf and swallowed his pill. Then he hurried to Ms. Satchel's cabin, quite forgetting the watch in his bathroom.

Walking to her door he couldn't help recalling the man who'd fled Ms. Satchel.

Even before he found her glasses, he sneezed. There was *something* in her cabin. It brought back a memory of his first — only — trip to a zoo. Snatching her glasses off the table, he hurried out of the cabin.

By the time he and Ms. Satchel entered the theater, he was only sniffling.

Afterward, he walked with her to her cabin. "Do you like monster movies?"

"Love them. Of course, I tend to side with the monster."

"You, too?"

"I never gave up hope that Frankenstein's monster would find a nice girl or that Dracula would discover he had a simple mineral deficiency." She opened her door and turned on the light. *"Blazes!"*

The cabin looked as if a convention of monsters had raged through it. Clothes were strewn all over, drawers littered the floor, and the mattress was tipped against a wall.

She pressed the button marked *Steward* and looked around at the wreckage.

Though Fortney didn't want to leave her at a time like this, he'd begun to sniffle, which, he felt, detracted from the seriousness of the moment. "I'll go see if the steward is coming."

As he shut the door behind him, he was shaken by a sneeze.

Heurtebise's door opened and the inspector, in an

olive paisley dressing gown, stepped out. "Do you know the time?"

"No."

"It is, boy, no hour to be prowling the corridors, waking decent passengers with shouts of *blazes* and great, hideous sneezes."

"I'm . . . waiting for help." Fortney stretched his upper lip over his teeth trying to stifle a second sneeze.

"I don't know what devilry you're planning, but you are to go directly to bed without any help. Is that clear?"

Pressing a finger over his upper lip, Fortney mumbled, "It's Ms. Satchel. Her cabin's wrecked."

"We shall see." As Heurtebise seized Fortney's arm, a stewardess passed them and knocked on Ms. Satchel's door.

Ms. Satchel opened it. "My cabin has been ransacked."

Towing Fortney, Heurtebise followed the stewardess inside. "That is evident, madame. Even Americans do not practice such housekeeping. Stewardess, you will undoubtedly find the purser cavorting at the Poseidon Party. Inform him, but discreetly, that Inspector Darius Heurtebise of the French Sûreté requires his presence here at once. And bring fresh linens." He urged her on her way, then examined the door and jamb. "Nothing forced. Nothing damaged. So our culprit let himself in with the door card for this

cabin." He gave Fortney's arm a jerk. "The card, boy."
He shut the door. "In your hurry to put things straight,
madame, you realize you are destroying fingerprints."

She shoved a drawer back into a chest. "In this day,
Inspector, even the most spontaneous burglars wear
gloves."

"No matter. I shall proceed by deduction. Open and
shut. When were you last in here, madame?"

"Just before dinner."

"I presume the cabin was intact. And *during* dinner
you sent the boy to fetch your glasses."

"Of course."

Fortney struggled to stifle a sneeze. He realized now
what it was in the cabin that made his eyes water and his
throat itch. The same feeling had assailed him at the
zoo, between the zebras and the ostriches.

Ms. Satchel pawed through a jewel box. "Nothing
seems to be missing. Where did you put that watch,
Fortney?"

His face felt as if he'd been scalded. "I . . . forgot it. I
think I left it in my bathroom."

There was a knock. Heurtebise admitted the purser
followed by the stewardess with folded sheets and pil-
lowcases.

"You are with the French Sûreté?" Baird seemed
overly impressed.

Heurtebise nodded. "At your service. We are faced
here, as you see, with an act of wanton vandalism."

Fortney sneezed.

Heurtebise fixed him with a gaze like a sword. "Not content with stealing Ms. Satchel's watch, that miserable creature wrought the havoc you see, hoping that ravishing the cabin would cover his theft. Look at the wretch. Sniveling. Eyes brimming. At least he can still feel guilt. It may mean there is yet some kernel of conscience in that sunken chest."

A chain of sneezes shook Fortney. Before another storm could strike, he gasped, "Horse. Feathers."

"*Horsefeathers?*" Heurtebise seemed to grow taller. "*Horsefeathers!* How dare you, boy! That is not only vulgar American slang, it is obsolete slang. Have you no sense of style, no respect for your own language?"

"The boy has allergies," Ms. Satchel reminded him. "Perhaps he's allergic to — "

"To *horse* feathers?"

"To horses, *and* to feathers," she said calmly.

"You are telling me, madame, that we are honored by the presence of a horse and a bird in this cabin?"

She turned to the stewardess, who was sliding a fresh case over a pillow. "That is a feather pillow?"

"Of course," Baird said. "We use synthetic fillings only if a passenger requests it."

"And Fortney's aunt requested synthetic?" Ms. Satchel asked.

"Synthetic everything," he said wearily. "Just before we sailed I had to assure her that all our carpets are synthetic, all our public rooms furnished with polyester upholstery and draperies. Believe me, we went to some trouble fitting her suite with the same at the last minute."

"So not *all* the passenger cabins have synthetics." Lifting the cushion from an overstuffed chair off the floor, Ms. Satchel tore from its edge something which she handed Heurtebise. "Read this."

" 'Do Not Remove This Tag Under Penalty of Law' — *Madame, what have you done?*"

Taking the tag from him, she went on, " 'This article contains all new materials, consisting of curled hair: cattle five percent, horse ten percent. . . .' Now, Fortney, you had better go take a pill. Mr. Baird, will you help the stewardess replace my mattress?"

"I will escort this boy to his suite and speak to his aunt," Heurtebise said. "Allergy or no allergy, he bears watching."

"The watch is id my bathroob," Fortney assured Ms. Satchel damply.

"That's perfectly all right. Don't worry about it," she said.

"Madame, you may be the single greatest obstacle to firm law enforcement that I have yet encountered." Heurtebise's hand closed like a steel claw on Fortney's shoulder. "You. Come along. And do not assault my ears with boggy syllables."

"I don't want a word of this to get out," Baird warned. "We mustn't upset the other passengers."

"There is no need to instruct me in procedure or proprieties, Mr. Baird," Heurtebise said. "I shall offer my services to the captain in the morning."

"That is neither necessary nor appropriate," Baird told him firmly.

"You will leave that decision to me. Come, boy. And no tricks. You would be hunted down like a dog."

He did not speak again until they were in Fortney's suite. "So. Empty. No supervision. That explains a great deal. I am going to find your aunt, and you are not to leave this room. Do you understand?"

Fortney nodded, sniffling.

After he took his pill, he sat on a chair waiting until Elena came.

She threw her wrap on a table. "Are you all right?"

"I didn't do it."

"Of course you didn't. Do you want to tell me about it?"

"No. But I didn't do anything."

CHAPTER FIVE

••• MORNING •••

He slept poorly. In the morning he said, "I don't think I want breakfast."

Elena came out of her room in a pale ivory dress. "The inspector, I should guess. They say you should force yourself to face your fears. *They*, whoever they are, specialize in advising others how to be miserable. Why don't we have breakfast sent up?"

Having breakfast in his sitting room with a view of the ocean restored his appetite considerably.

"If we watch carefully, we may see dolphins," Elena told him.

"Watch! I've got to give Ms. Satchel her watch! Will you come with me?"

As they were leaving the suite, their cabin steward, Frank, intercepted them to say they were wanted in the purser's office.

Heurtebise, standing beside Baird, nodded somberly to Elena as she entered the office with Fortney.

"Captain Carson," Baird murmured, "Mrs. D'Aubigne and Fortney Potter."

Standing with his back to an imposing desk, the

captain told Elena, "I understand Mrs. Sandal's cabin was vandalized last night and her watch stolen."

"Satchel," Elena said, "and her watch was not stolen. Fortney has it."

Wishing Elena had explained more fully *why* he had it, Fortney dug the watch out of his pocket. The inside of his throat itched.

As Carson reached for the watch, Heurtebise said, "No. No, Captain. Let him confront his victim himself and make restitution. It may impress him. But let him explain what he proposes to do about the wrecked cabin."

"Right. Right." Carson grew more severe. "What made you do it, son?"

"What possible reason would he have for doing such a thing?" Elena demanded.

"There is no reason to ask a reason," Heurtebise reasoned. "Boys are not reasonable."

Fortney cleared his throat. The first time it had itched this way was when he'd taken a bite of a friend's tuna sandwich.

"I understand you were creating a disturbance the first night, Fortney," Carson continued. "Several passengers complained."

"I saw a man running out of a suite," Fortney wheezed.

Carson's gaze was cold. "You're imaginative, I'll say that for you."

"And consumed with guilt," Heurtebise added.

"Look at him — chest heaving, tears in his eyes. Confess, boy. You'll be the better for it."

"There's something fishy here," Fortney gasped.

Carson scowled. "That is for us to say, young man."

"Fishy?" Heurtebise demanded. "Are you insulting my reasoning, my deductions?"

"He is allergic to fish," Elena said.

"Fish," Heurtebise informed her, "swim outside, in the sea."

She looked at the ivy on the desk behind Carson. "I assume you fertilize that plant, Mr. Baird."

"Like clockwork. Just this morning — "

"You fed it a fish-emulsion fertilizer," she said. "Gentlemen, good morning. I suggest you resume your investigation with more wit than prejudice."

Only Fortney's wheeze undermined the dignity of her exit. "Inhaler," he gasped in the corridor.

She hurried him to the elevator.

In his bathroom, he opened his medicine cabinet and seized the inhaler. He had arrayed the cabinet as he did the one at home: pill bottles and inhaler on the bottom shelf, eyedrops and cough lozenges tucked behind them.

After a few deep breaths, he told Elena, "I've got to give Ms. Satchel her watch."

"Are you sure you feel all right?"

"I've got to."

Ms. Satchel was not in her cabin, nor on the promenade deck. He looked in lounges, shops, the library, he walked around deck after deck.

Now and then he looked at the watch. As noon approached, he felt as if a murky, moss-lined cavern were opening inside his stomach.

He knew he would find Ms. Satchel at their table at lunch . . . along with Marais, Heurtebise, and probably Baird.

From the way he felt, he thought he would be legitimately sick by noon. He could stay on his sofa and ask his aunt to return the watch.

Heurtebise had insisted he return it himself.

Would Heurtebise and Baird make him do it himself?

Not likely. Fortney had no doubt that Elena was more than a match for them.

But if he asked her to return the watch, would she have trouble keeping her faith in him?

Would anybody with a clear conscience be afraid to return a watch?

Certainly, Heurtebise would take it as a confession.

Asking Elena to return it to Ms. Satchel privately after lunch was like an *announcement* of guilt.

Fortney realized he had no good choices open, only dreadful ones.

••• AFTERNOON •••

He went to lunch. And he was right. It was dreadful. Marais, Heurtebise, and Baird were all there. Nobody mentioned the night before. The longer nobody mentioned it, the more Fortney felt it as the silent focus around which all the polite talk eddied.

He wondered if anyone had told Marais what had happened.

He couldn't concentrate on the menu. He mumbled his order so that the waiter had to ask him twice to repeat it. He felt guilty ordering anything, because he didn't think he'd be able to eat, but he couldn't bring himself to sit at the table and order nothing. Somebody would be sure to ask why he didn't order. Everybody would know he was too upset to eat. Guilt, they'd assume.

He knew he could never bring himself to simply get up and leave the table. If he could last through lunch, he thought, he would follow Ms. Satchel and return the watch privately.

What if she asked him for it first? She might, at any moment.

What could he say then? How could he explain, in front of everybody at the table, why he sat with that watch in his pocket not offering it to her?

Baird and Marais were talking to Elena. Heurtebise was poking his crepe suspiciously with a fork.

Before another thought could strike, Fortney thrust the watch toward Ms. Satchel. He talked too fast, his voice sounded hoarse, and he wasn't sure it was loud enough to hear. "I really did forget it, twice."

"Of course you did," she said. "I cannot tell you how many watches I've left on bathroom shelves over the years. Why don't you hang on to this one until we dock?"

From the pause in the other conversations at the table, he knew she'd been overheard.

"For my sake, Fortney," she urged. "I don't think I can bear another two days of hearing you sniffle and wheeze and ask what time it is. Use the watch so you can take your pills *before* you need them."

He knew that, however long he lived, he would always love Gertrude Satchel.

He moved the food around his plate, and ate a few bites. When lunch was over, he left the dining room, the watch in his pocket, suffused with the solemn relief of one who has survived an ordeal in better shape than he'd anticipated.

In their suite, Elena said, "I'm going to make an appointment for a massage. Then why don't we go down to the pool?"

"I'd better take my pill."

He was at the desk in the sitting room drawing squiggles on the ship's heavy cream-colored stationery when she came out of the bedroom in a terry-cloth caftan, carrying a canvas tote bag. "Aren't you coming?"

"I . . . promised to write home."

"You could swim first."

"I don't know how." The confession was embarrassing, but he didn't want her to think he was just being cloddish. "At home, pools were around trees or grass."

"Then this is the place to learn. I'll teach you."

"I have to take a pill at two."

"Bring the watch."

"It might get wet. Besides, I'd better get this letter written."

"All right. May I borrow the watch? I'll come back before two to shower and change for my massage."

He handed it to her.

"Sure you won't be bored?" She put the watch in the tote.

"I'm sure. Have a good time."

When she'd gone, he wrote on a fresh page, "*Dear Mom and Dad. . . .*"

Then what? *I'm having an interesting time. I got a rash at dinner. Either I had a nightmare or I have hallucinations or a man who likes Elena is crazy. I am suspected of being a thief and a burglar. . . .*

"*This is a very big ship,*" he wrote.

Someone knocked.

He was tempted to sit still and wait. But what if it was Frank who'd forgotten to bring fresh towels or something earlier. What would the steward think on unlocking the door and finding him sitting at the desk?

He opened the door.

"I thought you and Elena might like to try some trap shooting," Marais said.

"*Trap* shooting?"

"Skeet shooting. Clay pigeons."

"Clay *pigeons*?"

"Simple clay disks, Fortney. Do you want to come?"

"Elena went swimming." Immediately, he regretted saying it. If Marais really couldn't remember a battle with a prowler, and losing two watches, there was no predicting what he might do. "I'd sure better hurry. I'm supposed to meet her. Late already. She's waiting."

"I won't keep you, then."

With Marais gone, there was nothing to do but go to the pool. It was serious enough being thought a liar and a criminal by Carson, Baird, and Heurtebise, without being caught in a lie by Marais.

His mother had packed new bathing trunks for him. He put them on, wishing she'd gotten a sensible color like black. Slipping into rubber thong sandals, he trudged out of the suite. He wondered if he should have brought a towel — then he realized he hadn't brought his door card.

Before he reached the elevator, the thong pulled out of the hole in the sole of the right sandal. He wondered if people were allowed on the pool deck barefoot. Would one working sandal count as not barefoot? He would look like a fool walking across any deck with one sandal flapping. He'd look more of a fool standing outside the door of his own suite until Elena returned.

He went down to the purser's office. Michael Baird was outside it, talking to a red-haired woman. When she walked away, laughing, he looked at Fortney. "Yes?"

"I forgot my door card, and my sandal broke."

Baird went into his office and came out with a thick rubber band. "Lift your foot."

Fortney did. "I suppose I'm not allowed on the pool deck with a broken sandal."

"I don't know why not." Baird put the band around Fortney's foot, sandal and all, and straightened up. "There. Now, in the future, I suggest you wear more than bathing trunks on your way to and from the pool. It's all right now. You go on and enjoy yourself. Just remember for the next time."

Fortney mumbled his thanks and scuffed away, wondering if there was any limit to the ways he could make himself feel stupid.

As he emerged on the pool deck, he saw Elena dive from the highest board and surface, swimming easily. A man so old his skin looked loose dived from the low board and sliced the water with barely a splash.

Fortney stood at the pool's edge. Two toddlers jumped in and bobbed up paddling like puppies. They looked like the kind who would splash people on purpose.

Elena grasped the pool's edge near his feet and smiled up at him. "Come on in." She swung easily out of the water. "All you do is stand — no, right at the edge — bend forward, and let yourself fall. You're not bending."

"I just remembered something. May I borrow your door card?"

"It's in the tote." She slid back into the water. "Be sure you don't go anywhere and lock me out."

It would have been easier if she'd looked disgusted.

He hadn't told Marais he was actually going to swim, he reminded himself. But he was not cheered. He knew he would grow up a wheezing, sneezing, itching, stunted recluse whose voice still cracked at thirty.

Stalking into his bathroom, he threw Elena's door card on the vanity and pulled the rubber band off his foot.

There was a white pill on the floor.

As he picked it up, he saw another by the shower stall.

He opened the medicine cabinet. The bottles and inhaler were a fraction of an inch out of line.

In all the years he had handled his own medicines, he had never had a bottle or an inhaler a hair out of line.

Carefully, he shut the cabinet door.

Kicking off the good sandal, he ran to the elevator. He made himself walk across the pool deck. He would say calmly to Elena, "It seems we had a prowler in our suite."

Before he was close enough to speak, she vaulted out of the water. "What is it?"

"Somebody . . . somebody was in our suite. Spilled my pills. . . ."

She picked up her tote bag and shrugged into her caftan. Like an avenging Amazon, she strode into the purser's office, Fortney following. "Tell him."

"Somebody was in our suite while we were . . . while Elena was swimming," Fortney told Baird.

"What did he look like?"

"I didn't see him."

"Uh huh." The purser looked at Elena and spoke as if Fortney did not exist. "Your door is tamper proof. It can be opened only by your own coded cards." He looked at Fortney. "I thought you'd left yours in your suite."

"He used mine," Elena said.

Baird smiled. "It seems to me that a nap may be all that's required here."

She turned away without speaking.

In the suite, she prowled like a cat, opening doors and drawers, even stepping into closets. "Everything seems all right. And your card was right here."

"But *somebody* spilled my pills."

"Do you have an extra bottle?"

"There were just a couple of pills on the floor. Somebody must have been looking behind the bottles. A steward sure as heck wouldn't be doing that."

"Why would anybody be opening your pill bottles?"

"I didn't say anybody opened them."

"Then how did they get spilled?"

"They have child-proof caps. I never get them back on right."

"Don't you know pills *degenerate* if you leave the tops off?"

"Not off. Loose."

"Loose, too."

"We're talking about somebody creeping around in my bathroom!"

She spoke with care. "You are. What I am going to do is shower quickly, change rapidly, and get my massage, and then find Gerard or someone else who is not going to frazzle me any further. You may amuse yourself however you like, so long as you do not create a disturbance of any major proportion on this ship."

He stalked into his bathroom and took his two o'clock pill, reflecting bitterly that it was at least half an hour late. Then he showered, hoping to disturb the water pressure in her shower.

Dressing in the steamy bathroom, he breathed silently and easily. Maybe he should spend the rest of the trip in the shower, he reflected. Of course, she'd accuse him of letting his pills *degenerate* from the damp.

He came out of his bathroom just as she strode from her bedroom. She put the watch on the desk. "Have a good afternoon. Remember your pills. And your door card."

When she'd gone, he reminded himself that he was safely shut in with the door card on his desk.

As it had been when someone got into his bathroom.

He carefully folded his four o'clock and six o'clock pills in a tissue, put it in his pocket, then, with the watch and door card in his other pocket, he left the suite.

The ship, so fabulous the day before, seemed bereft of anything worth doing. There was no point in visiting a sauna after a shower. He didn't play billiards. He'd probably be told to leave the card room. If he bought anything at a shop, Elena could say, "I see you got over your mood."

He wandered into the library. There were two people in there, women older than Ms. Satchel. They glanced up as if they expected him to make noise.

He walked between the rows of books. As he came to the end of each aisle, the women eyed him apprehensively.

Taking *The Short Stories of Edgar Allan Poe* from a shelf, he sat in a chair which was set squarely against a wall, facing the only door. He took out the watch. Three-thirty. Over four hours until dinner.

As soon as he'd started reading, he knew he'd made a mistake. *The Tell-Tale Heart* was too terrifying to enjoy and too engrossing to set aside.

"It's four o'clock."

The sepulchral voice came from one of the women.

"Teatime," she added.

"I believe I'll stay here and finish this chapter," the other said. "It's about Lady Hamilton and Lord Nelson."

"Everybody's known about *them* for decades. And we're paying for tea."

"I get palpitations."

"From reading that nonsense?"

"From the tea. It must be the caffeine. You run along."

He was relieved that one of them stayed. He was not ready to be left alone in a library with Poe.

••• EVENING •••

He'd finished *The Masque of the Red Death* and was well into *The Cask of Amontillado* when the woman who'd gone to tea returned.

"You're late," the other woman greeted her.

"Late? How can I be late? I never said when I'd be back."

"It's six o'clock. Tea does not last until six anywhere in the world. You must have swilled it by the pot. Diabetes, that's what you're headed for."

"And who was it downed three petits fours at lunch?"

He found their bickering rather a relief. Too much Poe was like watching Creature Features until dawn.

"Ah. Fortney Potter."

He looked up. It was Ms. Satchel.

"So you're a reader, too." Pulling a chair close to his, she sat down. "I can resist a library for only a few days. Then I have to enter, if only to admire the titles." She glanced at his book. "Ah. Poe. Always gives me the creeps. Especially *The Murders in the Rue Morgue*. Have you had tea?"

"No."

"I hope you eat a decent dinner. You barely touched your lunch. I remember how wretched I felt during my hunger strike in prison."

There was a silence in the library.

"Prison?" he breathed.

"A very small one."

"What for?" he ventured, as the other women sat motionless.

"I was not going to *eat* in prison when I objected to being there," Ms. Satchel said reasonably.

"I mean, how did you get there?"

"I was arrested."

"For what?"

"A bad sense of direction. I was heading for an out-of-the-way village for my lessons and I crossed a border by mistake."

"What were you teaching?"

"Oh, they were teaching me. The language of the drums, how to move safely among serpents, a bit of healing. . . . What time is it?"

He took the watch from his pocket. "Seven-fifteen."

"I must be going."

"Ms. Satchel," he blurted, before he could change his mind, "there was a prowler in our suite this afternoon."

The older women glanced at each other wildly, briefly.

"So! Two in two days." Ms. Satchel stood. "Should I come up there with you? We might pick up a clue."

"That's a good idea."

In the elevator, she said, "Tell me more about the prowler."

He did.

At the door of the Imperial Suite, he hesitated. While he could not imagine entering alone, there was something he had to know. "You're not just humoring me, are you?"

She considered for a moment. "To some extent. But, since there was a prowler in my cabin, it seems quite reasonable to think there was one in yours."

"Thank you." He took out the card. "Ready?"

"Yes."

"Let's stand back so we're not in the way of anybody leaving." He opened the door. *"Well, I guess it's time to be getting ready for dinner."*

"It's past time, and why are you shouting?" His aunt came out of her room in a long dress the color of sea foam. "How are you, Ms. Satchel?"

"Running a bit late. I'll meet you both at dinner."

"Are you wheezing?" Elena asked him when Ms. Satchel had gone.

"I forgot — I forgot my four o'clock and six o'clock pills!"

"That's marvelous! If you were able to forget them, then you didn't need them."

"Now that I've thought of them, I need them."

As he headed for his bathroom, Elena said, "You're not going to take them *now*?"

"Just my eight o'clock pill." He swallowed it. "I'd better bring my inhaler and plenty of Kleenex, though."

He came out, stuffing his pockets.

"You look as if you're going on safari," Elena observed. "Let me put some of that equipment in my purse."

As he handed her the watch and the inhaler, there was a knock at the door.

"That's probably Gerard," she said.

Fortney followed her out, reaching behind him to be sure their door was shut tight.

Marais' gaze swept from Elena's hair to her feet and back again. "Ondine," he murmured.

"Unseen?" Fortney asked nervously. "What?"

"Ondine." Marais kept looking at Elena as they walked. "Ondine is a naiad."

"An *eye* ad?" Fortney followed them into the elevator.

"No, no. A naiad. A water sprite." Marais ushered Elena out of the elevator as if she were exquisitely fragile. "Your aunt looks like a water sprite tonight." He smiled as Ms. Satchel came out of the adjoining elevator. "Ah, Ms. Satchel — how splendid you look."

"But not like a sea nymph." Ms. Satchel entered the dining room with them. "A dugong, perhaps — dugongs were taken for mermaids by the sailors of classic Greece."

"What is a dugong?" Fortney asked cautiously.

"It's like a manatee." She greeted Heurtebise and Baird.

"Manatee." While Fortney was unwilling to display his ignorance, he had found that Ms. Satchel's explanations were often more interesting than her original statement. "That's not like in *hu*manity?"

"No. The manatee is also called a sea cow, a peaceful, vegetarian sea mammal with weak front flippers and no hind flippers. It's on the verge of extinction — that's its only relation to humanity."

"How do you mean?"

"It doesn't dislike humans enough to evade us. I used to watch manatees from an island off the West Indies. Ungraceful, but so endearing."

"You seem to love islands," Marais observed.

"They hold a fascination for me, as well," Heurtebise admitted. "Devil's Island, especially."

Ms. Satchel looked aghast. "That infamous penal colony?"

"It should never have been abandoned." He eyed his poached salmon as if it were some unwholesome relic, washed up in a sitting room. "Those who disturb society should be removed from society. What a golden age we might enter if all boys between six and sixteen were transported to an isolated, but decent island and provided with humane keepers and adequate plumbing. Food, medical necessities, and proper literature would be dropped by helicopter — "

"Speaking of food," Ms. Satchel intervened firmly,

"I've not seen Mr. Arnold since the night he ran from me. Avoiding me is one thing, but to drop from sight entirely does seem an overreaction. I've even knocked on his door to see if he might need anything, but there's no sound, no sign of life from his cabin. The stewardess won't tell me anything."

"Ship personnel never discuss one passenger with another," Baird said.

"But the man could be sick, even suffering!" she protested.

"Now, that *is* an overreaction," he chided.

"How do you know?" she demanded.

Baird turned his attention to his meal.

"Really — how do you know?" she persisted.

"I saw him. Will you be coming to the Caribbean Carnival tonight, Fortney?"

"But when did you see Mr. Arnold?" Ms. Satchel pressed.

"At teatime — in the library." Baird turned his attention back to Fortney. "I never saw anybody look so solemn over a carnival. I promise it will be worth your while. Why don't you all come as my special guests?"

Fortney looked at the tablecloth. He had been in that library from 3:30 until 7:15. Either the purser was careless about the time, the day, or the truth, or there was something far worse happening. If there had been someone else in the library, maybe there *hadn't* been anyone spilling pills in his bathroom; maybe nobody had run out of Marais' suite. Was it possible to have positive and negative hallucinations? Could he ask Elena? What if she had to find him a psychiatrist? Did French psychiatrists speak English?

"Fortney? Did you hear Mr. Baird?"

Fortney looked across at Elena. "I was . . . thinking."

"Plotting, more likely, " Heurtebise murmured.

Elena ignored him. "Fortney, why don't we go to the carnival tonight? There was no floor show at the First Night Follies and you missed the Poseidon Party last night."

He'd never been to a carnival. They were always held at fairgrounds near weedy fields with dusty parking lots.

Besides, he thought he'd better not act strange, in case he wasn't. He didn't want to know what might happen to a twelve-year-old who began cracking up aboard this ship.

The Caribbean Carnival was not what he'd expected. No side shows, no rides, no cotton candy. Only hundreds of people sitting at tables while a pale baritone in tight trousers and a blue ruffled shirt sang "I Did It My Way."

The dancers who came onstage next perspired heavily and clenched their teeth as they smiled, but Fortney occupied himself with trying to count the colors in their costumes.

He was not eager to see the ventriloquist and dummy, who were next, but, to his relief, the dummy had no apparent injuries. By not watching the ventriloquist's lips move, Fortney could almost enjoy the performance.

After them came the comedian. His hair was so shiny, it looked painted on, and his shirt had more ruffles than the singer's, and his first jokes were about bathrooms.

The mountain climbers, at a nearby table, laughed heartily at every joke. "If I did not revere the law," Heurtebise muttered, "I would make my way to the hold and file the points off their pitons."

"Off their pythons?" Killing snakes seemed to Fortney a bizarre and brutal act.

"Pitons," Ms. Satchel said. "Spikes used in mountain climbing. A rope goes through a hole in one end, and the other end, which is sharp, is jammed into rock crevices."

A waiter hurried to Baird and bent to whisper in his ear. Everyone at the table kept watching the stage so as not to seem to be eavesdropping.

Baird stood. "I'm sorry. Policy decision. Enjoy yourselves." He threaded his way between tables in the waiter's wake.

Ms. Satchel nudged Fortney. "What did the waiter tell him?"

"The ventriloquist's dummy said the dancers moved like a chain gang, so they threw him overboard."

Heurtebise stood. "Homicide. Justifiable, but still homicide. I will be needed."

"The dummy. They threw the dummy," Fortney explained. The ventriloquist is threatening to dive after it if they don't stop the ship."

"That would be the decent thing to do," Ms. Satchel murmured.

"Diving after the dummy?" Marais asked.

"Stopping the ship." She toyed with a carrot stick. "I assume it would float."

Heurtebise glanced at her in surprise. "The ship?"

"The dummy." She stood. "I'm afraid this floor show has nowhere to go but down, and, even more unfortunate, on. Good night. Sleep well, everyone."

Within a few minutes, it was clear that she was right.

"Are you ready to go?" Elena asked Fortney.

"Oh, yes."

Marais stood. "Good decision."

Heurtebise got to his feet. "I do not intend to sit here alone with hearty mountain-climbing Neanderthals only tables away." He got in the elevator with the others and rode up to the signal deck. "Madame D'Aubigne, you have ignored my presence all evening. This is unfair. When I speak of the brute, barbarous nature of boys, I am merely stating facts."

"Inspector," she said wearily, "I find your opinions both contentious and ageist."

"Madame, opinions are not contagious, and my religious convictions are no concern of yours."

"Contentious, not contagious," Marais told him. "She means you argue about everything."

"Ageist, not atheist," Elena added. "You are unspeakable toward Fortney because he is young."

Bristling, Heurtebise followed them from the elevator. "I merely maintain that once society recognizes the twisted mentalities of boys, it will be better equipped to deal with them."

Elena unlocked her door. "Good night, gentlemen."

Even before she stepped into their suite, Fortney said, "I smell a rat!"

She switched on the light.

The sitting room looked as if a troupe of elephants had performed a ballet in it.

"Stand back! Don't move!" Squeezing past Fortney, Heurtebise threw open the bathroom door, looked into the closet, then hurried into the bedroom.

"Nothing," he called. "Come in."

"Inhaler," Fortney wheezed.

Heurtebise came out of Elena's room. "This, boy, has gotten beyond mere mischief."

"Don't badger him, Inspector." Uncorking the inhaler, Elena handed it to Fortney.

"Badger? Is it possible to badger a child so depraved he destroys his own quarters to divert suspicion?"

"Divert suspicion?" Marais asked.

"He ransacked Ms. Satchel's cabin only last night."

"He did not," Elena snapped. "This afternoon while we were swimming there was someone in here."

"I suppose this boy observed that from the pool. *What is he doing?*"

"He is inhaling asthma medicine," she said coldly.

Snatching the inhaler from Fortney, Heurtebise sniffed at it. "Ha!"

Elena took it from him and handed it back to Fortney. "It is prescribed medication."

Heurtebise narrowed his eyes. "Does it not seem strange to you that he takes these seizures whenever he is accused? It is guilt — that's what you're seeing."

Corking his inhaler, Fortney shook his head. "Rat. . . ."

The inspector's voice dropped to the rumble of a waking volcano. "*You are calling me a rat?*"

"He is not." Elena's voice was icy. "He means a rat is making him wheeze."

"Oh, madame." Heurtebise regarded her with pity and dismay. "A rat did this?" He opened the door. "One-inch steel deadbolt. Nothing tampered with. Madame, how would a rat hold a door card in his tiny claws?"

She was unmoved. "If Fortney says he smells a rat, he smells a rat."

"Madame, this is the fastest, most highly advanced ship ever built. Everything is new, immaculate."

"As a matter of fact," Marais observed thoughtfully, "rats can be a problem on the finest, cleanest ships. Even on this marvel, one might find a few in the hold."

Heurtebise spoke with great care. "The hold is twelve decks below us. You are telling me this boy smells a rodent twelve decks down?"

Elena did not falter. "No. Someone from the hold has been in here."

The inspector's voice was edged with the most exquisite fatigue. "Carrying a rat. A parrot on the shoulder would have been so much more picturesque."

"My nephew is so sensitive to allergens he would wheeze if a person who had been frequenting the haunts of rats had been in here."

Fortney coughed.

"Shouldn't you take a pill or something?" Marais asked.

Fortney shook his head. "It'll go away," he gasped.

"What? What did he say?" Heurtebise asked.

"It sounded like 'little stowaway,' " Marais ventured.

"Of course! A stowaway!" Elena seemed so relieved Fortney could not bring himself to contradict her.

"Stowaway," Marais echoed slowly.

"Perhaps we should eliminate the world's police forces," Heurtebise suggested. "This boy could solve crime, not by deduction, not by investigation, but by allergy. He could form his own Interpol — "

"He, at least, has an open mind," Elena countered.

Once more, Heurtebise opened the door. "I wash my hands of you all. Fini. I would suggest you ring for a steward, unless you are accustomed to sleeping in such disorder. In the morning, I shall report to the captain. Let him probe this boy's unlatched mind."

CHAPTER SIX

••• MORNING •••

"After last night, we deserve to have breakfast sent up," Elena decided.

Fortney couldn't eat.

At eleven, Frank, their steward, knocked and asked them to come to the captain's office.

This, at least, was an expected ordeal. Fortney put his noon pills and his inhaler in his pocket. "Where's the watch?" he asked anxiously.

"I'll bring it," Elena assured him.

Captain Carson, standing behind a great gleaming monument of a desk, motioned them toward a black sofa where Heurtebise sat.

Fortney perched at the end, as far as possible from the inspector, with Elena between them. Baird, arms folded, stood next to a painting of a sailing ship.

"I assume the inspector told you our suite was ransacked," Elena began.

"He did." Seating himself, Carson scanned a lined yellow pad on his desk. "As you opened your door last night, even before you turned on the light, your nephew announced, 'I smell a rat.' Now, how did he know anything was wrong *before* the light was on?"

Elena was calm. "He didn't say anything was wrong. He said, 'I smell a rat.'"

"And what does 'I smell a rat' mean, Fortney?" the captain demanded.

Fortney cleared his throat. "It means I smelled a rat."

Carson gripped the edge of the desk as if trying to anchor himself. "You mean a *rat*? A rat in our Imperial Suite? You are flirting with libel. This ship is swept, scrubbed, scoured, sterilized, fumigated. . . ."

Fortney tried to breathe quietly. He knew what was making his throat itch and his chest feel squashed, but he was held in awful fascination by the captain's rage.

Carson leaned forward. "We treat our guests as royalty. We pamper them, treasure them, protect them — *unless they threaten the safety or the morale of this ship.*"

"One moment." Heurtebise lifted a hand. "Let us proceed point by point. Now, boy, you claim you smelled an actual rat upon entering your suite."

Coughing, Fortney nodded.

"And how do you know?" the inspector persisted. "What makes you so certain you recognize the aroma of rat?"

"When I was four," Fortney wheezed, "our nursery school had a pet rat. I had to drop out."

"And you mean to tell us you have *remembered* that

rodent's reek for eight years?" the inspector thundered.

"When Fortney has a serious asthma attack," Elena asserted, "it is memorable."

"Is this whistling when he breathes supposed to be funny?" Carson growled.

"It's a play for sympathy." Heurtebise glowered at Fortney. "*Will* you stop squirming around this sofa like a newt, boy?"

"Dog on it," Fortney wheezed.

The inspector's glare would have immobilized a dervish. "Doggone it? You may well say 'doggone it,' boy, for there is no way out. The only thing for you to do is confess."

"He *said* 'Dog on it.' " Elena's voice was cold as her gaze. "He is allergic to dogs."

"Ah. Well. That explains everything." Heurtebise patted the sofa cushions. "St. Bernard? Terrier? Hound? Sitting somewhere between us? Curled up on my lap?"

She ignored him. "Captain, you have had a dog in here."

"Madame, pets are never allowed in cabins," Heurtebise assured her.

"There is not a hair on that sofa," Carson snapped. "It was vacuumed just after Admiral went back to the kennel."

"Admiral?" Heurtebise asked.

"My bulldog," Carson explained. "We don't consider

him a pet, but a mascot. When the sea air gets nippy, he sleeps on the sofa, but it was vacuumed — WHAT IS THAT BOY DOING?"

"He is using his inhaler because your dog sleeps on this sofa." Elena stood. "Come, Fortney."

Carson, too, stood. "Get him and that . . . impaler . . . out of here, Mrs. D'Aubigne, but keep an eye on him. *The boy must be controlled.*"

The inspector followed Fortney and Elena from the captain's office. In the corridor, he said, "You could not have seen that dog, Fortney Potter. *I* have never seen that dog."

He edged into the elevator with them and pressed a button. "You are either a budding criminal genius or a possessor of a nose any hound might envy. One way or another, boy, you do indeed bear watching."

As the elevator door opened, he took Fortney's arm. "Come. You must learn proper breathing." He guided Fortney onto the sports deck and watched him collapse in a chair. "You must inhale from the abdomen . . . so." He sucked in a great whoof of air and let it out with an explosive *hah*. "Proper breathing, proper habits, proper diet. Come. It's almost lunchtime."

Fortney took another whiff from his inhaler.

••• AFTERNOON •••

"Come, boy. You can't skulk out here unfed. Skulking is the first step toward loitering." Hauling Fortney to his feet, Heurtebise took Elena's arm. "Self-discipline, Madame D'Aubigne, is the secret of a useful life. Moderation in all things. Sound mind in a sound body."

He urged them into the dining room with a salvo of inspiring commands. "Shoulders back, boy. Chin up. Appearances! Appearances." Pausing only to greet Ms. Satchel and Marais, he seated Elena and Fortney, with himself between them. "Take charge of your life, Fortney Potter. No slouching. No nonsense." He summoned a waiter, ordered for himself, and then said, "Bring this boy a proper meal. He must build himself up. Muffins.

"No nut muffins," Fortney demurred.

"Very well. No nuts. The boy will have strong tea. Ham. Trout."

"No meat, no fish," Fortney interrupted with a firmness that surprised him. "I will have onion soup and salad."

Heurtebise gazed at him somberly. "I said self-discipline, boy, not self-sacrifice."

"It's no sacrifice," Fortney insisted.

"Of course not," Ms. Satchel agreed. "I've not eaten fish, flesh, nor fowl for fifty years. Not since I was almost a sacrifice, myself. I was kept in a bamboo cage, fed dreadful slop, and scheduled to be roasted in a volcano. It gave me a new insight on the eating of other creatures."

"Volcano." Heurtebise gazed at the plate the waiter

set before him as if it had offered an unspeakable insult. "A most effective place to dispose of evidence."

"And bodies," she observed. "Concrete blocks are so unimaginative."

"That was the sort of thing I had to contend with, the sort of thing which drove me near retirement. Dreary, uninspired crimes." Heurtebise crumbled a cracker over his soup. "Eat your muffins, boy."

Fortney obeyed.

There was a small sweet spurt as his teeth met in the muffin.

"You must learn to eat properly," Heurtebise advised him. "Exercise, study, improve your mind. Drink strong tea. Tannic acid clears the blood. Don't sit there like a lump with your mouth full, boy! Swallow."

Fortney knew he was making a mistake, but there was no other way to dispose of that bite of muffin under the fearsome gaze of Darius Heurtebise.

He swallowed.

Ms. Satchel smiled nostalgically. "I was always saying that to Lavalier."

"Saying what?" Heurtebise asked.

"Don't sit there like a lump with your mouth full, boy," she murmured.

"I'm not." Fortney stifled the urge to scratch his shoulder blades against the chair back.

"Not you," she assured him. "Lavalier was always sitting around like a lump with his mouth full."

"Lavalier — isn't that a pendant?" Marais asked her.

"I suppose he was dependent, for a caiman. He was injured when I found him, but I was able to return him to the river in time."

Fortney was torn between awe and a frantic need to scratch. "You found a *caveman*?"

"No, no." She speared an escarole leaf. "A caiman. A crocodilian. Like an alligator."

Heurtebise scowled. "*Will* you stop squirming, boy? Finish your muffin."

Fortney tried to sit still. "It's the berries."

Heurtebise lifted his eyes toward the ceiling. "Don't you know any modern slang, boy? Has all your education come from the reading of outmoded trash novels? 'It's the berries' was a vulgar expression of approval fifty years ago."

Fortney took the pill bottle from his pocket. "Blueberry muffin." Shaking out a pill, he swallowed it with a gulp of bitter tea.

Ms. Satchel pushed back her chair. "Why don't we walk around the deck, Fortney? Later, I will show you my new mystery novel." To the others, she said, "You will excuse us."

But Marais and Baird were busy talking to Elena.

On deck, Ms. Satchel asked, "How soon does the pill work?"

"It should start soon."

"Good." She sat on a deck chair. "When did you first hear that you had allergies?"

He sat in the adjoining chair, scratching his back

against the canvas. "I've had them as long as I can remember."

"So for as long as you remember, you've heard you had allergies. And, of course, you believe it."

"Don't tell me it's all in my head," he implored. "That's what my grandparents say."

"Nobody knows what's in another creature's mind. I'm just thinking that once you're convinced berries give you a rash, a taste of berry might be enough to make you itch. If you're convinced birds cause your asthma, the stirring of a feather could start you wheezing. But what would happen if you could change what you believe?"

"How?"

"How do you think of me?"

"I think you're wonderful."

"That's because I know I'm a fascinating woman who has lived for many years. But to *change* a belief takes attention."

"Like repeating, 'I don't have allergies'?"

"That would merely be arguing with yourself. You must relax, where nothing will intrude, and picture yourself as you wish to be. You must not strain. When you start changing to match your picture, you may add details. You might picture yourself feeding a friendly rat."

The purser passed, a woman holding on to his arm as if he were something won at a fair.

Ms. Satchel got to her feet. "Mr. Baird."

He and the woman turned.

"I cannot help worrying about Mr. Arnold," Ms. Satchel said. "I've still not seen him at a meal."

"I'll keep an eye out for him." Baird smiled as the woman flicked his neck with her scarf. "What does he look like?"

"You saw him in the library only yesterday," Ms. Satchel reminded him.

"Of course. I'll keep an eye out for him." He walked on, murmuring something to the woman attached to his arm.

Ms. Satchel was still staring after him as Heurtebise and Marais approached. "That man!" she huffed.

Heurtebise stopped. "I assure you, madame, I had no idea it was a berry muffin. I came to see how the boy is."

"I mean the purser," she said. "He said he saw Mr. Arnold at teatime in the library yesterday, and just now he asked me what Mr. Arnold looks like."

"It's pretty creepy," Fortney said in a low voice.

She turned her attention to him. "What is?"

"I was in the library from three to seven yesterday," he confided hesitantly, "and I didn't see any man in there. This ship . . . this ship is hard on the nerves."

Heurtebise looked at him quizzically.

Ms. Satchel's voice was stern. "I think our purser is either fuddled, or trying to placate me as if I were a fool, Fortney. For all we know, Mr. Arnold has been tossing on a bed of pain all this time. I will ask the captain to send for the waiter assigned to Mr. Arnold's table. We'll see if he came to any meals. The cabin steward will know whether he has had food sent in. Will you come, Inspector? You may be useful."

Left with Marais, Fortney said, "Well. I have to get some letters written."

"Good idea." Marais fell into step beside him.

Fortney did not want to risk being alone in an elevator with a man who either lied about prowlers and watches or forgot about them. If he should go crazy in a small place, he would be hard to avoid.

Fortney made for the staircase, muttering, "Great exercise, stairs. Use them all the time." Marais followed.

By the time they reached the signal deck, Fortney was breathing hard and wondering if twelve-year-olds could have heart attacks. The walk down the corridor seemed like a slowed film, but at last he reached his door. Touching the card to it, he realized that anything might be inside, waiting.

Marais opened the door. With his hand against Fortney's back, he urged him into the suite and shut the door behind them.

"Sit down, Fortney. It's time we had a talk."

Between him and the door was Marais. Behind, windows only a steward could open. Over his upper lip was a moustache of sweat. "Talk. Glad to. Maybe after I finish my letters."

Marais stepped toward him. "The inspector seemed to believe you about Arnold's not being in the library. What else have you and Heurtebise talked about?"

"Allergies." It sounded to Fortney like the crackling of a dead leaf.

"Have you discussed me, or the man who was in my suite?"

"That was a dream."

"Don't be funny." Marais stepped closer. He took a billfold from his pocket, flipped it open, and held it toward Fortney. The card behind the plastic window was pale cream, with raised chocolate lettering.

SHABANDAR
IMPORT-EXPORT

New York-London   *Gerard Marais*
Paris-Amsterdam   *Representative*

Fortney stepped back.

"Where do I start? The export business is only my cover, Fortney."

"Cover?"

"I'm a government agent."

"Oh. Uh . . . what government?"

"Ours, man! I'm on undercover assignment. That's

why I had to deny there was anyone in my suite. Luckily, he didn't get it."

"Get what?" Fortney whispered, afraid to sit down, but feeling strange and shaky.

"The watch!"

"Which . . . which watch?"

"The one he was after! He was trying to get it off my wrist when I woke."

The thing to do was pay attention and act polite and interested. "He should have known that would wake you."

"Not if I'd been drugged."

"*Drugged?*" Involuntarily, Fortney backed toward the window.

"If I'd been drugged, he could slip my watch off, slip a duplicate on my wrist, and I'd never know. Fortunately, our friend Heurtebise got the drug that was meant for me."

"He did?" In spite of his unease, Fortney was beginning to be intrigued.

Marais sat on the edge of the desk. "Of course. Remember the First Night Follies, when the mountain climber's cheese fell in the inspector's glass? I gave him my mineral water and got another. And the next morning Heurtebise said he'd slept as if he'd been drugged."

"But the inspector didn't act strange that night."

"Fortney, only in films do drugs take immediate effect. There were probably a few sleeping pills dissolved in my drink."

"By who?"

"Whom."

"What?"

"*Whom*, not *who*. It could have been anyone. There were hundreds of people around us. We can be sure, though, that anyone who saw me give Heurtebise my drink wasn't in on it."

"Only you and I and he and Elena saw."

"Precisely. And, thinking I had drunk the drugged water, someone sneaked into my suite."

"So if you hadn't accidentally switched glasses you wouldn't have your watch. . . ." He looked at Marais' wrist.

"I don't."

Fortney wondered how long it took for secret agents to be able to cope with complications like this.

"You do," Marais said.

Fortney's skull seemed to be expanding and contracting. He felt sick.

"Pay attention. Not being drugged, naturally I woke when someone tried to take the watch off my wrist. He was as surprised as I, but he put up a decent fight. I knew, of course, they'd have to make another try. So I hid it."

"*The* watch?"

"Right. In Ms. Satchel's tape recorder, when I got her sweater for her the next morning. Who would think of looking in an eccentric old woman's recorder?"

"She's not so eccentric."

"I planned to recover it just before we docked, but either the watch slipped around or something else was wrong with her recorder. I never figured on her taking the machine apart and finding the watch. You and she have been driving me crazy, flashing it around, passing it around — who has it now?"

"Elena."

"*Wearing* it?"

"It's in her purse. I've got to tell her!"

"Has anybody seen her with it? Has she taken it out in front of anyone?"

"No. But what if she — "

"Fortney! Be calm. *I* haven't been able to keep track of the blasted watch. They're not going to attack anybody unless it's their last and only chance, and certainly not until the last possible minute. They got a scare when that drug failed."

"*They?*"

"The man who ran from my suite — have you seen him before or since?"

"No."

"Neither have I. So someone else drugged my drink. And whoever got into my suite, whoever got in here, and into Ms. Satchel's cabin, either has cards that open these doors, or an accomplice who does . . . *and* some way of knowing Ms. Satchel had the watch, and knowing she gave it to you."

Fortney's stomach felt like a hollow ball, flopping and

twisting as air leaked from it. "We'd better go find Elena."

"Fortney, *she must not know anything.* If she knew, she would be in great danger."

"Why?"

"Because that's the way it works. So long as you and she seem harmless and ignorant, that's your protection. I am running this mission, Fortney. I would take it very, very seriously if you did anything to endanger it. Now, as soon as we dock at Southampton, you'll give Ms. Satchel back the duplicate watch, the watch the prowler dropped, and give me the real watch. You and Elena will sail to Cherbourg the next morning, Ms. Satchel will go on to London, and you need never think about it again. Meanwhile, you're doing a great service to your country."

"Where is it?"

"Your *country?*"

"The duplicate watch."

"In the ship's safe."

"Well, why didn't you put the real one there in the first place?"

"Fortney, how many people keep their wristwatches locked up in a safe?"

"You put the copy in there."

"Try, just try, to understand. When I boarded this ship, I had no idea anyone aboard even knew about the real watch. I didn't want to call *attention* to it by putting it in a safe. I was to keep that watch on me at all times. And believe me, no safe would slow down the people who want that watch. Now, obviously, since they tried to steal the real watch, it's too late for me *not* to attract attention. So I put the duplicate in the safe."

"That must be some watch. And I wish I'd never met it."

"The less you know about that watch, the better off you are. But your job, now, is to find out for me what Ms. Satchel has learned about the missing passenger."

"Mr. Arnold?"

"He may figure in this, somehow. Find Ms. Satchel. Ask her if she'll have tea with us. Then ask innocently about Mr. Arnold."

"What about Elena?"

"I'll go find her now. Don't look so worried. I'm trained for this sort of thing." He opened the door. "I'll bring her to the sports deck. Meet us there."

After a haphazard search for Ms. Satchel, Fortney went to see if she might have returned to her cabin.

He found her standing outside Mr. Arnold's door, along with Heurtebise, Captain Carson, and a stewardess. Fortney edged closer.

"You say the bed's never been slept in, no meals sent in?" Carson asked the stewardess.

"Nothing, so far as I know, sir. Every day when I go in to straighten up, nothing's been touched. Suitcase has been lying open on the bed since the first night.

Soap has never been unwrapped, nor a towel used."

"Knock once more," Carson directed.

Fortney drew closer.

"All right. Open the door," the captain told the stewardess.

Carson and Heurtebise entered the cabin, followed by Ms. Satchel and the stewardess. Fortney stood in the doorway.

The inspector opened a closet. "Suit, jacket, trousers." He looked through the suitcase on the bed. "Shirts, socks, underclothes. So. Our Monsieur Arnold boarded, hung up those garments which would wrinkle unacceptably in the suitcase . . . and then what?"

"He left this cabin that night, fled me, and has never been seen at table, never returned to finish unpacking, to bathe, eat, or sleep," Ms. Satchel concluded.

Carson smiled. "I see you read mystery novels, Mrs. Parcel."

"I write them," she said.

Standing in the doorway, Fortney sniffled. He'd had the same feeling in his nose the day his Grandfather Royce gave him a football.

Heurtebise turned. "You. Come in here and stop lurking about. Why are you sniveling? You've not been accused of anything."

Fortney stepped inside the cabin and sneezed. "Pigskin," he explained.

The inspector's eyes narrowed to dark slits of menace. All his former cordiality vanished. *"Pig's kin!*

Impertinent wretch! Just whom are you calling a pig's kin?"

"Not pig's kin," Ms. Satchel interposed. "Pigskin."

"Ah, *pig*skin! There is, perhaps, a wild boar in our midst. We have a canvas suitcase on the bed. We have suit, jacket, all cloth, in the closet. But somewhere in this room, unknown to us all, a swine lies unobserved."

"You didn't check the closet shelf," Ms. Satchel said.

Flicking her with a glance of weary disdain, Heurtebise went to the closet and, reaching over his head, felt along the shelf. "Ah." He took down a briefcase. "Well. We may find a passport, some identification." He unzipped the case. "Hah. Why would the man bring an empty briefcase? *Will* you stop that loathesome sniveling, boy?"

"A pigskin briefcase, no doubt," Ms. Satchel observed. "I find the use of leather articles unspeakably barbaric. Mr. Arnold is plainly a man of no sensitivity, no taste."

"And possibly no existence," Heurtebise added.

"True. I should not speak ill of the misplaced. If he fell overboard, or was propelled, it could have happened any time after I saw him."

"No." Carson looked solemn. "You said Mr. Baird saw him the next afternoon in the library."

"I said Mr. Baird *claimed* to have seen him." Ms. Satchel's voice was firm. "According to Fortney, there was no man in the library at that time."

Carson glanced at Fortney as he might an insignificant but repellent insect. "At any rate, all we can do now is institute an inquiry." He strode from the cabin, the others following. "I do not want a word of this to get out. The other passengers must not be alarmed. Stewardess, secure that door, then have the first officer and communications and security officers sent to my quarters."

Fortney sneezed.

"Where are your pills?" Heurtebise demanded.

"In my pocket."

The inspector took his arm. "Come. We will have tea and you will take your pill. Madame Satchel, you will join us?"

"Of course," she said.

As they walked to the elevator, Fortney protested, "I'm supposed to meet Mr. Marais on the sports deck. To . . . to maybe play shuffleboard or something."

"Boards," Heurtebise pronounced, "are meant to be built with, not shuffled. And you, boy, are either diabolically clever, or the greatest talent I have come across in law enforcement. Whatever the case, I will not have you skulking about unescorted. There are sinister things aboard here. Something is rotten in the state of Denmark!"

Fortney had no choice but to enter the elevator. "I don't think we're near Denmark."

Heurtebise pressed the button for the sports deck. "Have you never seen *Hamlet*, boy? Act one, scene four — as Hamlet follows his father's ghost, Marcellus says, 'Something is rotten in the state of Denmark!' "

"Why?"

"Because when a dead king's ghost walks about, it is evident that something is awry, is it not?"

Fortney repressed a shudder. "He was rotten?"

Ms. Satchel pried Heurtebise's fingers off Fortney's shoulder. " 'Something is rotten in the state of Denmark' means that something strange and suspicious is going on, Fortney."

Heurtebise glowered down at him. "How can you have lived twelve years in ignorance of the bard?"

"What barge?" Fortney stammered.

"Bard," Ms. Satchel explained, "is another word for poet."

"Just as boy is another word for barbarian." Heurtebise nudged Fortney out of the elevator.

"There's Mr. Marais, with my aunt. I'd better go."

The inspector seized Fortney's arm in an unrelenting grip. "They will have tea with us like civilized people, rather than abusers of boards."

As Marais and Elena came toward them, Ms. Satchel murmured, "It's going to be awkward sitting at tea and not telling them about Mr. Arnold."

"But of course we'll tell them," Heurtebise said.

"The captain instructed us not to discuss it," she reminded him.

"Discuss what?" Marais asked.

"Not with anyone who knows nothing of it." Heurtebise nodded to Elena. "But Monsieur Marais knew we were going to the captain. And Madame D'Aubigne's suite has been vandalized." Heurtebise offered Elena his arm. "Come to tea. We will tell you everything."

They did, and he did.

So there was nothing left for Fortney to report to Marais.

"I am baffled and unnerved, and my scones are cold." Ms. Satchel looked depressed. "Invaded cabins, missing passengers — do they all form some sinister pattern?"

"How could they?" Elena asked. "None of us had met before this trip, except Fortney and I. And with all the burglaries, nothing is missing."

"Except Mr. Arnold." Ms. Satchel crumbled a scone. "So we are the only passengers who have any idea what is happening. And we have no inkling of why it's happening."

"With Captain Carson convinced Fortney is the culprit," Heurtebise said, "we must rely on ourselves for protection. And now, I suggest we rest before dinner. Who knows what this night may bring?"

"What a splendid line." Ms. Satchel beamed. "May I use that in my next book?"

••• EVENING •••

At the door of Fortney's and Elena's suite, Marais said, "Do you mind if I check it out?"

As he looked in closets and behind doors, Elena said, "You know, this is ridiculous. We might as well be on some savage frontier."

"A frontier where they dress for dinner, however. I'll come back for you just before eight. Be sure you're on time, Fortney. On time." He looked at Fortney for a long moment, then left.

"Do you still have the watch?" Fortney asked Elena.

"Oh, lord, I'd forgotten all about it."

She fished the watch from her purse.

"Be sure you bring it to dinner."

"Of course. I'm as aware of your pill schedule as you are. I'll put it in my evening bag now."

At six-thirty, Ms. Satchel brought him the manuscript of the mystery novel she was writing. "Tell me what you think of it. I must hurry back. I left the inspector guarding my cabin."

"*I awoke to find myself haunted,*" her book began.

He read on, against his better judgment.

As they walked to the elevator at eight, Marais said, "I hope I didn't come for you too early."

"Elena has our watch," Fortney said.

"It's around eight." She didn't open her purse.

They were already seated when Heurtebise and Ms. Satchel joined them.

"It's going to be awkward with Michael Baird at our table," Ms. Satchel murmured. "By now he certainly knows I went to the captain."

"He's not going to bring it up," Heurtebise assured

her. "In the first place, it would be too embarrassing. In the second place, Captain Carson told us not to discuss Monsieur Arnold, and undoubtedly the purser was told the same."

The inspector was right. Baird greeted them politely, and talked about the weather, the ocean, stamp collecting, and salad dressings.

"We're having the Final Fiesta in the Baroque Lounge tonight," he said after dinner. "Dancing, floor show. . . ."

"The same floor show as the First Night Follies, Poseidon Party, and Caribbean Carnival?" Marais asked.

"And mountain climbers to throw cheese in one's drink," Heurtebise added.

"I think I'll go to the concert in the Lobelia Lounge," Elena said gently.

"Tonight's movie," Fortney told Ms. Satchel hopefully, "is about a ship that turns upside down and catches fire in an earthquake after it's bitten by a shark that's under control of aliens from another galaxy."

"It sounds . . . overwhelming," she conceded, "but they're playing Brahms at the concert."

Heurtebise fixed Fortney with a piercing glance. "I understand that your primitive nature will not permit you to appreciate good music, boy. However, the rest of us possess enough taste and sensibility to preclude our viewing that ghastly film. Therefore — "

"I'll go with Fortney," Marais offered.

Elena took out the watch. "It's nine-fifteen. Suppose we all meet in the Lobelia Lounge at eleven-forty."

Fortney and Marais sat at the back of the theater, four rows behind the nearest people.

At the first dull moment in the film, Fortney whispered, "How well?"

Marais inclined his head. "How well what?"

"How well trained?"

"Who?"

"You. You said you were trained for this sort of thing."

"What sort of thing?"

"I don't know. You said it. I thought you meant dangerous secret missions. Do you use karate or hidden weapons or mind control or what?"

"Everything," Marais whispered.

A man four rows ahead of them turned around. "Shh!"

Fortney watched the film until the explosions died down and the volcano rested and the shark took a break.

"It doesn't seem right," he whispered.

"What doesn't?"

"Just sitting here."

"Nothing we can do, Fortney, until we reach Southampton. In the morning I want you to get the watch from Elena. I'll give you the duplicate to return to Ms. Satchel just before we dock. We'll all go ashore together — even Heurtebise. Safety in numbers. Then you'll slip me the real watch, and go on to France the next day. Meanwhile, Elena's safe in the Lobelia Lounge, and I'll see you both locked in your suite for the night. . . . You didn't tell me there was a brontosaurus in this film."

After the dinosaur and the shark and the supporting actors were destroyed and the stars saved, Fortney and Marais went to the Lobelia Lounge. Sincere-looking men and women in black were departing with cellos and violins. At a small table near the back of the room, Heurtebise sat with Elena and Ms. Satchel.

"So," he greeted Fortney. "I assume the film was brutal enough for you? You know, of course, that the average film is designed for twelve-year-old viewers. That is, for the most depraved, demented. . . ."

"Inspector," Elena warned.

He looked injured. "Why do you block my every effort to communicate with the boy? I am trying to converse with him about something he enjoys, film."

"I remember filming a firewalking festival in Fiji," Ms. Satchel reminisced. "My film went up in flames as twenty islanders crossed ten ells of glowing coals."

Heurtebise looked impressed. "And the poet Dante mentions only nine hells."

"Ells," she repeated. "Ten ells. About thirty-eight feet."

Fortney's stomach seemed to slip to one side. "Who lost two feet?"

"Nobody." Ms. Satchel spoke as if to a respected

colleague. "An ell is a measure of distance." She glanced up as the purser approached.

"How was the Brahms?" he asked.

"Brahms gives me a brief illusion of hope for the species." Heurtebise looked past Baird at the mountain climbers entering the lounge.

"Incidentally," Baird told Elena, "the captain has instructed me to have the night steward keep an eye on your corridor tonight."

"To keep prowlers out or the boy in?" Heurtebise inquired.

Baird looked at him coolly. "Since you and Ms. Satchel saw fit to go to the captain this afternoon, perhaps you know better than I."

"A night steward for Madame D'Aubigne's only protection?" Heurtebise was unabashed.

"Our facilities are strained," Baird said. "The ventriloquist locked the dancers out of their dressing room. He's in there with their costumes, and they hear cloth tearing. They want to break down their dressing room door and throw him overboard, but we're attempting to persuade them to wait until we're nearer port. On top of that, a dock strike has Southampton all but paralyzed."

"And who is to guard Madame Satchel's corridor?" Heurtebise persisted.

Baird smiled thinly. "With you across the hall, how could she be safer, Inspector?"

"Fortney and I will be perfectly all right," Elena said.

"Who is going to invade a suite with two people in it?"

"You have not read Poe," Heurtebise informed her somberly. *"The Murders in the Rue Morgue."*

"But in that tale, the killer was a gorilla," Ms. Satchel pointed out. "I'm sure a gorilla among the passengers would have been noticed by now."

"I am not so certain." Heurtebise looked at the mountain climbers who sat at a nearby table with their maps. "At any rate, I would not take this lightly, madame. There is no guarantee the culprit will not return to the scene of his first crime — your cabin."

"I know," she said. "I wouldn't miss it for the world."

"Maybe we could all stay up and play cards." While he could not sound even faintly amused, Fortney struggled to appear casual.

"Cards, boy? Next it will be roulette, then hanging about gambling dens, borrowing to cover losses. . . ."

Elena took the watch from her purse. "It's late. Will you excuse us?"

A waiter, face pale and damp, dashed into the lounge. "It's the comedian," he blurted, even before he reached Baird. "Broke into the galley! Tried to arm the dancers!"

Baird sprang to his feet.

"We have him cornered," the waiter panted, "but he's got all the shish-kebab skewers."

Ms. Satchel watched Baird and the waiter sprint from the room. The climbers, engrossed in their maps, didn't look up.

She stood. "Come, Inspector. It may be a long night."

As she passed the table around which the climbers sat, she paused.

"We'll make base camp here. . . ." Their leader, Kurt, the blond, tanned climber, glanced up as Ms. Satchel peered over his shoulder.

"I'm afraid that won't do at all," she observed.

"Ah, ma'am," Kurt said, "this is a map of — "

"Oh, I know the map. But I know the mountain better." Reaching over his shoulder, she put her finger on the paper. "It was precisely here that an avalanche deposited me *here*." She moved her finger a fraction of an inch to the left. "Lost my gear, and two toes to frostbite. Impossible terrain. But it is possible to make a better approach." She looked around her for a chair. "Let me show you."

Marais accompanied Fortney and Elena to their door.

"It wouldn't hurt to . . . ah . . . check the closets and all. Probably proper precautions." Somehow, Fortney got the words out untangled.

"Good point," Marais agreed.

Fortney watched him and Elena recklessly peering behind doors. The draperies hung in neat, symmetrical lines across his window. He imagined how it might be to see a massive bulge behind them, hear a muffled snarl. For a moment, he imagined they moved slightly, imagined he felt the faintest breeze. He reminded himself that the window could only be opened from the inside, and only by a steward.

When Marais had gone, Fortney asked Elena, "How many people were in that Rue Morgue the gorilla invaded?"

"Two."

"I suppose a gorilla could tear the door right off the hinges."

"Given a choice, any sane gorilla will avoid people." She glanced at him, then carried a blue chair to the door and wedged it under the knob. "Try to sleep."

She turned off the light. Fortney wondered how a chair would deter a beast which could fling doors around like playing cards.

"Anyway," she said from the bedroom, "it didn't come through a door. I think it climbed up a wall."

By the time he was convinced he would lie awake all night, he fell asleep.

CHAPTER SEVEN

SOUTHAMPTON

He awoke, wheezing, to the smell of rats and . . . "Elena!"

As the light in her room went on, he scrambled out of his bed. "Elena! Elena!"

He collided with her in her bedroom.

There was a banging in the corridor and Marais' voice: "Elena!"

Snatching her robe off a chair, she strode into the sitting room. Even in his panic, Fortney remembered his country. Seizing her evening bag from her dresser, he ran after her.

She switched on the sitting-room light.

"Steward!" Marais was shouting. "Get this door open!"

Hauling the chair from under the knob, she unlocked the door. As she opened it, Marais drew her quickly into the corridor. Frank, the steward, pulled Fortney out.

"There's something. . . ." Fortney gasped.

Passengers in robes and pajamas were spilling into the corridor.

96

"Stand back." Shouldering Marais aside, Frank charged into the suite and slammed the door behind him.

Marais tried the knob and muttered something.

The passengers shifted like cattle before a thunderstorm.

"Wait a minute," Elena said. "How? How would anybody get in that suite? The only entrance was locked from the inside with a chair under the knob."

"But there is!" Fortney wheezed. "There's something in there!"

He heard the passengers muttering.

"There's something in there!"

"Isn't there supposed to be anything in there?"

"I saw the steward go in there."

At last, the door of the suite opened and Frank stepped into the crowded corridor. "There's nobody in there."

Elena put her arm around Fortney's shoulders as if to shield him from the crowd. "Come on. You need your inhaler."

Fortney didn't move. "It has to be in there. How could it get out?"

"It couldn't," Frank said flatly.

"If it didn't get out, it's *in* there," Fortney insisted desperately.

"What is?" Elena asked.

"I don't know. I smelled a rat and — "

"Did he say a rat?"

"*A rat could start a plague!*"

". . . and cats. . . ." Fortney's wheeze was lost in the passengers' uproar.

"Please! Everybody! Be calm!" Frank shouted.

"There's nothing to worry about! The boy had a nightmare!" Seizing Fortney's arm, Marais hauled him into the suite, Elena following close behind.

She locked the door and leaned her back against it.

Fortney could hear the cries in the corridor.

"*Bats? Bats start a plane?*"

"*Vampire bats?*"

"*Plague! There's a plague!*"

Then, over all the voices, one, electric with rage and authority: "Back! Back, I say! To your quarters!"

As the pandemonium outside died to a sullen rumble, the door shivered under a great blow. "Open up! This is your captain!"

Wordlessly, Elena obeyed.

Like some stone idol come to life, Carson lurched in, jacket misbuttoned, gleaming shoes trailing untied laces. "*I am wakened at this unholy hour. 'Riot on the signal deck, Captain!' I rush to the scene. I find MUTINY among the first-class passengers! WHAT HAVE YOU DONE, FORTNEY POTTER?*"

"He thought there was a rat in here," Frank explained.

Kneeling on his bed, Fortney fumbled under his pillow. "And cat fur."

"What? What did he say?" Carson demanded.

"Something about cat burr," Frank ventured.

"*Cat* burr?" Carson repeated.

Elena's eyes widened. "Cat burglar?"

"A cat burglar on my ship?" The captain's rage was mixed with incredulity.

Fortney uncorked the inhaler, even though he feared that using it now might seem disrespectful, even provocative.

"You are trying to tell me someone climbed up the side of my ship in mid-ocean?" Carson sat heavily on the foot of Fortney's bed.

"They climb up buildings," Elena pointed out.

"There is nothing under or around this ship but ocean," Carson remonstrated.

"There's nothing around buildings but ground . . . or concrete . . . both of which are harder than water," she said.

"So a cat burglar sprang from the depths of the sea, scaled deck after deck of a moving ship to enter a suite through a window that cannot be opened from the outside." Carson turned his glare on Fortney. "STOP WHISTLING!"

"That's wheezing," Elena said.

"What is it, boy?" Haggard, Carson moved the inhaler aside with the back of his hand. "Did I do you such unspeakable harm in a past life that you have returned to destroy me? Are tales of the Flying Dutchman more than legend? Are you some demon doomed to drive simple seafarers to degradation, desperation, despair?"

As Fortney tried to bring the inhaler back to his lips, Carson caught his wrist in a grip like that of a drowning man. "Whether this latest outrage was a play for attention, pure demented malice, or something even darker, you will not succeed!" He stood unsteadily. "We dock at Southampton in less than twelve hours. I have a missing passenger, guerilla war among my entertainers, and a deck of berserk passengers. Now. I will tell you only once, Mrs. D'Aubigne. *Keep this creature under control!* Is that clear? He is not to show his soppy nose before we reach Southampton."

"I assume he will be allowed ashore at that time," Elena said coldly.

Carson turned. "Oh, yes. By all means. I will spend the day in silent prayer that, by some miracle, you will miss our sailing to Cherbourg."

Frank sprang to open the door.

"Try to get some sleep, Elena." Without a glance at Fortney, Marais followed the captain and Frank out.

Before she went to her room, Elena asked, "Do you need anything, Fortney?"

"No."

He had brought more shame than he could fathom on himself, made the voyage a horror, lost Marais' trust and respect. But overriding all this was fear.

Something had been in this suite. Something which smelled of rats and cats, which entered and left through locked doors and fled the light.

Fortney lay awake until gray light seeped in to wash

out the dark, certain he would never sleep without fear again.

He woke when Elena came into his room and pulled the cord beside the window to open his draperies. "Do you know what you want for breakfast?"

He blinked at the light. "Not much."

He helped her make his bed into a sofa again.

When breakfast came, neither of them ate or spoke much.

"Might as well pack what we won't be using today," she said, after she finished her coffee. "We'll stay in Southampton until after dinner, and be in Cherbourg tomorrow."

It took him only a few minutes to pack. Then he read more of Ms. Satchel's book. Had he not been haunted by a real terror, he would have found it deliciously fearsome.

Between pages ninety and ninety-one, he found a handwritten note: *"By now, Fortney, you realize what a masterful tale I've created. But it's not much compared with the glory and intricacy of creating one's own life. What I was trying to say on deck yesterday was that you create your life, and your self, every moment. Within every situation, every moment, at the point where myriad lives, things, problems touch you, you are choosing to what extent you participate in your own creation."*

Elena asked him twice what he wanted for lunch.

Moments after she ordered, there was a knock. It was Marais, with two suitcases. "I'll eat with Fortney while you go down to the dining room. I've ordered my meal sent here."

"You didn't have to do that," Elena protested.

"There's no sense in both of you being confined to quarters. Go enjoy your lunch."

She hesitated. "I've already ordered it sent up."

"I'll cancel it for you." He smiled. "You can distract the mountain climbers. They're driving Heurtebise crazy hanging around Ms. Satchel, asking her advice. Unless you divert them, she'll never be packed by the time we dock."

Fortney handed Elena the manuscript. "Will you give it to her? Tell her — tell her it's wonderful."

••• AFTERNOON •••

With Elena gone, Fortney said, "We'd better cancel her lunch."

"No. Let it look as if there are three people here." Marais took a watch from his pocket. "I got it from the safe."

Fortney jumped as the waiter knocked on the door. He watched three meals set out on the coffee table, thinking it was wrong but rather exciting to waste food so casually.

When the waiter left, Marais said, "We'll switch the

watches now. Heurtebise and Ms. Satchel are meeting us here so we can all go ashore together and share a taxi."

"What if *they* think Ms. Satchel or I still have the real watch?"

"They know I'm not going to leave you before I have it back. Once we've separated, I'm the only one in danger. Where is it?"

"It was in Elena's evening bag the last I saw."

"Get it."

"I don't feel right taking things from her purse."

Marais set down his fork. "You are not taking, you are exchanging a dangerous item for a safe one." He put the duplicate watch in Fortney's hand. "Do it."

Fortney saw neither the real watch nor Elena's bag in her room. He put the duplicate in his pocket. Feeling ashamed and sneaky, he opened drawers, and finally the suitcases on her bed. He knew she wouldn't pack her evening bag with the watch in it, but he wanted to be able to tell Marais he'd looked everywhere. The evening bag, empty, was in the largest suitcase.

He returned to Marais. "Her evening bag is empty. I looked everywhere. Maybe she put the watch in here."

"Why?"

"So I'd remember to take my noon pill."

As they searched the sitting room, Fortney said, "If she put it on a table or something last night it . . . *he* . . . could have grabbed it."

"Sit down!" Marais scrambled back to the sofa with

Fortney, just as Elena opened the door. "That was fast," he told her.

"Ms. Satchel is eager to get ashore and through customs."

"Good. Are you ready?"

"I have to get a few things." She went to her room.

"What time is it, Elena?" Marais nudged Fortney.

"About one." She came out with a jacket and purse.

Fortney stood. "I'd better give Ms. Satchel her watch." The duplicate felt heavy in his pocket.

"I did," she said.

"*When?*" Fortney demanded.

"At lunch."

"Why did you do that?" He felt his face get hot.

"You know how I am with watches. I didn't want to forget it and have to come right back to this wretched ship, or mail it to her."

"What if she loses it? What if somebody steals it?" His voice sounded squeaky and desperate to him.

She stood in front of the coffee table. "What is the matter with you? It's her watch. She's surrounded by mountain climbers and an inspector of the Sûreté. And who would want the tacky thing, anyway?"

"Just relax a minute." As Marais stood, coffee cup in hand, his shin bumped the table. Coffee sloshed down the front of her dress. "Elena! I'm sorry! Are you all right?"

"Merely wet. I will go change."

Setting down the cup, he called after her, "We'll go tell the others you'll be late."

"Don't wait for me." Her voice, from the bedroom, was controlled but tight. "I will come ashore when I'm ready. I will find a quiet spot in which to brood, and when my nerves improve to merely shattered, I will meet you outside customs."

Picking up his suitcases, Marais nudged Fortney ahead of him.

"Everything," he raged, herding Fortney toward the elevators, "everything is falling apart. Get down to Ms. Satchel. Ask to borrow the watch. I'll meet you at the end of her corridor. Hurry!"

Fortney ran ahead to the elevator.

As he edged around the passengers in the corridor on Ms. Satchel's deck, he saw her come out of her cabin and hurry away.

People blocked his sight as he went after her. When he glimpsed her again she was near the end of the corridor. As he scrambled to catch up, he saw Frank step out from a side hall. "Ms. Satchel? Security sent me. We'll take a service elevator."

She nodded. "When the security officer called, he only said they'd found Mr. Arnold. Is he. . . ."

"I don't know," Frank said.

"He said to come to Storage Shed Twenty-three. That sounds ominous."

"Can you hurry, ma'am? The inspector is waiting."

"I must leave word for my friends."

"I'll take care of that and bring your luggage after I take you ashore."

Fortney followed, hesitant to interrupt, more hesitant to risk getting in trouble for being out of his suite. Still, they were docked by now. And he couldn't return to Marais without the watch.

He sneezed. Ms. Satchel, his nose assured him, was wearing cotton. And he'd forgotten his noon pill.

She turned. "Ah, Fortney. How fortunate. Tell your aunt and Gerard that Inspector Heurtebise and I had to go ashore."

"You were not to say a word to anyone!" Frank interrupted fiercely.

"I know. I know. Your security man warned me. But Fortney's aunt expects us at her suite. I don't want her to think we've simply disappeared. Tell her, Fortney, if we're not at customs in half an hour, to go on."

She took out the watch. "It's one-thirty now."

He sneezed again.

"Did you forget your pills?"

He nodded.

She handed him the watch. "Keep this. A memento."

As he looked at it, stunned, Frank said, "You come with us, boy."

"Don't be ridiculous." Ms. Satchel sounded exasperated.

"He'll have to. You weren't to speak to anyone, and you've told him — "

"I've told him nothing that will do the slightest harm. If he comes ashore now, his aunt won't know where any of us are. She'll be worried sick."

"The inspector wants him to come," Frank insisted doggedly.

"I know what the inspector wants; he wants to exploit the boy's allergies. I can identify Mr. Arnold; Fortney can't. If more is required, the inspector and I will use deduction and intelligence instead of this boy's snuffly nose. Go back to your aunt, Fortney."

"Thank you." Clutching the watch, Fortney backed away hastily. "Thank you."

As Frank started after him, Ms. Satchel caught the steward's sleeve. "Where are you going?"

"I'll take the boy to his aunt."

"He is perfectly capable of finding her. And I am not prepared to find my way through a maze of lower decks and storage sheds alone. Go along, Fortney."

Fortney turned and hurried back along the main corridor. When he was halfway to the end, a hand fell on his shoulder from behind.

He turned.

"Come with me," Frank said. Then he looked at something behind Fortney. His hand dropped. Without another word, he wheeled and hurried away.

Fortney was turned around again by an even firmer hand. "Why are you not in your suite?" Heurtebise demanded. "Did your snuffling become too much for your aunt's nerves?" He knocked on Ms. Satchel's door. "Madame? Are you ready?"

Fortney wondered if the whole ship had been in-fected by some mind-altering plague. Maybe something in the ventilation system. "She went to meet you," he reminded Heurtebise politely, and sniffled. Heurtebise, he realized miserably, was also wearing cotton.

Ignoring him, the inspector knocked again. "Madame?"

"She just left to meet you."

"Stop that snuffling."

"I can't help it. You're wearing wool and cotton," Fortney replied.

Heurtebise glared at him. "I am in no mood for nonsense. I have been telephoned by some security person who said the ventriloquist was cutting loose the lifeboats. Then I was not *allowed* near the lifeboats, I found no ventriloquist, no commotion. . . . Madame! Are you in there?" He looked down at Fortney again with sudden steely suspicion. "Did you tell her to meet me somewhere else, wretch?"

"I just told you, she's going ashore to meet you, remember?"

Heurtebise shook him sharply. "Are you not quite bright, or do you think I am not? She is to meet me right here and go up to your suite."

Fortney clutched the watch harder.

"What have you got there?"

Fortney tightened his fist, but the inspector seized his wrist in a merciless grip and pried relentlessly at his fingers. Fortney resisted, but the inspector's wool jacket was only inches from his nose. As a monstrous sneeze shook Fortney, Heurtebise forced open his fist. *"What is this?"*

"A watch."

"Madame Satchel's watch, *n'est-ce pas?* I saw your aunt return it to her at lunch. Demon! How in the name of all that's evil did you get your wizened claws on it?"

"She gave it to me."

"Don't compound your crime with lies. Where is she?"

"She went ashore. Please give me my watch."

"Ha!" Putting the watch in his jacket pocket, Heurtebise transferred his grip to Fortney's upper arm. "Where's your aunt, then?"

"She may have gone ashore by now."

"We shall see."

"There you are!" Marais strode toward them. "I came to find out what was delaying you." He glanced sharply at Fortney. "Everyone ready?"

"Ready?" Heurtebise exploded. "Madame Satchel is missing!"

Fortney remembered his country. "Frank was taking her to Storage Shed Twenty-three to meet the inspector."

"I was called up to the boat deck on some fool errand," Heurtebise said. "I got back to find this creature hanging around and her gone. The boy is up to something."

"Inspector, you were not to meet her ashore?" Marais asked.

"Of course not. You know where we were to meet."

Marais' voice was urgent. "Fortney, *do you have the time?*"

"No. I. . . ."

Leaving his bags, Marais ran back toward the elevators.

"So! Now you've sent two people on a wild goose hunt!" Heurtebise tightened his hold on Fortney's arm.

"Let me go! I have to tell him something! Give me the watch, please!"

"I'm not releasing you until I find what's at the root of this madness. Pick up that suitcase. Marais is an idiot, but I'm not going to leave his luggage for some thief."

As they headed toward the elevators, Kurt, the climber, intercepted them. "We just discovered the dock strike has spread to the porters. I thought I'd better give Ms. Satchel a hand with her luggage. Is she still in her cabin?"

"No." Still gripping Fortney, Heurtebise paused only briefly. "But if you see her, send her to the Imperial Suite at once."

Elena was still in the suite.

Setting down Marais' suitcase, Heurtebise showed her the watch. "Did I, or did I not, see you return this to Ms. Satchel at lunch, madame?"

"Of course."

"Then how did your nephew get it? He had it outside her cabin, told me she'd gone ashore to meet *me*, and sent Monsieur Marais scurrying to look for her."

"She told me she had to meet the inspector at a storage shed," Fortney insisted.

Elena looked bewildered.

"Don't you believe me?" he cried.

"I'm trying. Oh, I am trying. But I'm still reeling from last night."

"He committed another atrocity last night?" Heurtebise asked.

"I don't want to go into it," she said wearily.

"Something was in here last night," Fortney insisted hotly, "and nobody believes anything I say!"

"Look, Fortney. *Look.*" Striding to the window, she seized the blue chair, hauled it to the door, and shoved it under the knob. "This chair was under this knob, *so.* When you shouted, I rushed out, pulled this chair away — *so* — opened the door, *so.* Oh. Kurt."

The blond climber stood in the doorway. "Is something wrong?"

"No, no."

"I was wondering whether Ms. Satchel had turned up here."

"No." She turned to Fortney. "Where was I?"

"Throwing chairs."

Glaring at him, she moved to pick up the blue chair.

Kurt stepped inside. "Let me." He lifted the chair. "Where does it go?"

"Against the wall," she told him.

"In front of the window," Fortney said.

She narrowed her eyes at her nephew. "It has always been against that wall."

"You took it from in front of the window just now," he reminded her.

"I don't care if it goes *through* the window." Stalking to the desk, she picked up the telephone. "This is Ms. D'Aubigne. Will you page Ms. Gertrude Satchel, please. It's urgent. Ask her to come to the Imperial Suite at once." She hung up and turned to the inspector. "If she is on board, she will come here. If she is not, she is ashore. Since Gerard is supposed to be scouring some storage shed, I shall look for her at customs. If none of us finds her, I suggest you keep my nephew out of my sight, or you will see a crime that will restore your faith in the quality of crime."

She left.

Looking as embarrassed as anybody trapped in a family fight, Kurt carried the chair to the window. "Did you do that, or did she?"

"Do what?" Fortney asked.

"Punch a hole under the sill. Stuffing paper in is no way to hide it. Somebody's sure to notice."

"I didn't!" Fortney went to the window. The paper handkerchiefs stuffed in the hole blended with the white wall, camouflaging the hole.

"So. Attempting to scuttle the vessel, now, boy?" Heurtebise gazed at the hole.

"Looks as if someone drove in a piton." Kurt set the

chair where it had been — in front of the window and the hole. He glanced at Fortney. "What's the matter?"

Fortney moved the chair aside. "If a piton was jammed in there with a rope hung out the window, somebody could climb up the side of the ship?"

Kurt smiled. "I don't know why anyone would want to."

"But someone *could?*" Fortney sneezed.

"With the piton driven right under the sill like that, yes. But — "

"Fortney Potter," Heurtebise said, "I alternate between horror at your depravity and awe at your criminal ingenuity. You're trying to make us believe someone climbed up a rope and in this window?"

"Please. Please, Inspector, listen. With the window open just enough so someone could get his fingers in, and with the draperies shut, there'd barely be a breeze. Last night, I thought I saw the draperies move and thought I felt a breath of air. Everybody said the windows could only be opened from the inside by a steward, so I thought I imagined it."

"The part of the boat deck directly below this suite is closed to the public," Heurtebise reminded him.

"Exactly!" Fortney wheezed. "He probably sneaked into one of the lifeboats, after dark, and when the rope dropped, tied it to part of the boat."

Kurt looked confused. "He?"

"The cat burglar!" Fortney turned to Heurtebise. "He must have sneaked up from the hold to the boat deck. He saw our lights go on when we came in, and when our lights went out, he knew we'd gone to bed. He waited a while for us to fall asleep, then climbed up the rope, and worked the window all the way open, got in, and I yelled, Elena and I ran out, and he must have climbed back down the rope."

"First," Heurtebise said, "why would he wait for you to return to your suite before invading — unless he was after something you had with you? Second, how would he manage to depart by window and take the rope and piton with him? If he left by the door, he would encounter the steward assigned to keep an eye on the corridor. Third, who could get in here with a rope and piton and open a window only a steward could open?"

"*Steward!*" Fortney breathed. "When Elena and I ran out, Frank came in and shut the door behind him. Then he came out and told us the suite was empty. Suppose *he* fixed the rope and piton while we were at the movie, and the concert! If I *hadn't* wakened, the cat burglar could have left by the door, with the rope and piton, because Frank was out in the corridor. But when I yelled, the burglar climbed out the window, and then Frank rushed in and threw the rope and piton overboard, stuffed the hole, put the chair in front of the hole to hide it when the draperies were opened. Inspector! Frank was going to take Ms. Satchel ashore, and he tried to get me to come with him!"

"Boy," Heurtebise said in a chilling voice, "either you possess a criminal brain dwarfing those of Attila,

Ghengis Khan, Bluebeard, and the perpetrators of every political scandal in history, or something *is* rotten."

Fortney sneezed.

"My wool and cotton?" the inspector asked.

Fortney nodded.

Heurtebise gripped his shoulders. "And do you recall what Ms. Satchel is wearing?"

"Cotton."

"Ah! Kurt, wait here in case Ms. Satchel appears. Come, boy."

Fortney sniffled. "I've got to get something for my allergy."

"Only handkerchiefs. No pills! And hurry."

Fortney rushed into his bathroom. Sneezing, he stuffed his pockets with tissues from the dispenser on the wall.

As he hurried to the elevators with Heurtebise, the inspector warned, "If this is some fantasy you've concocted, I will see that you pay a hideous price."

Baird emerged from the middle elevator. "I heard Ms. Satchel paged. Is something wrong?"

"Possibly. I was to meet her at her cabin, but the boy says she was taken to a storage shed."

"Shed Twenty-three," Fortney put in.

"The steward for this deck, Frank, may be involved. Have the ship searched for him and Ms. Satchel. Notify the Southampton police, and have the decks cordoned off. Then meet me at Shed Twenty-three."

Baird nodded. "I'll notify the captain. Fortney can come with me."

"I need his nose."

"You can't take him into possible danger," Baird protested.

"I can not leave a woman in more serious danger. You get to the captain."

The purser hesitated only a moment. "All right. Meet me in the dining room. We can get ashore faster through the galley." He stepped back in the elevator as the door closed.

Fortney and Heurtebise took the next elevator down.

They waited only moments in the empty dining room before Baird appeared. He unlocked the door to the galley and led them through pantries and storage rooms. "We set up a ramp here so we could smuggle the ventriloquist off without the dancers spotting him."

They stepped ashore, into eerie desolation. Around them was no sign of life, no movement, only what seemed like mile after mile of gigantic storage sheds with corrugated roofs.

"The pier is deserted!" Heurtebise exclaimed. "Something is rotten in the state of Denmark."

"It's the strike," Baird said. "Dock workers off a week, nothing loaded or unloaded, half of it not in containers. There'll be plenty rotten in the state of England soon. You'd have to walk all the way down to customs to see a living soul."

"Unfortunate for commerce, a stroke of luck for us. It should be simple to seal off the area."

Heurtebise peered at a building. "Shed Thirteen. So Twenty-three should be to our right."

Fortney sneezed.

"Stop that!" Heurtebise snapped.

Fortney stumbled after him. "It's your wool and cotton."

The inspector halted. "This is not going to work. I brought you to track Ms. Satchel's cotton frock with your invincible nose. However, I am not prepared to pursue the quest stripped to my nylon undergarments. Nor am I willing to have our approach heralded by your ghastly explosions."

"We can't let him wander out here alone," Baird protested.

"Indeed not. I would fear for the waterfront." Hauling Fortney into Shed Seventeen, Heurtebise backed him into a narrow space between two enormous containers. "Keep your scraggy frame wedged out of sight. If you move a foot from this spot, I will see that you regret it to the end of your days."

Fortney sneezed.

"This is ridiculous!" Baird growled.

"He'll stop as soon as I leave," Heurtebise assured him. "When the police come, we'll foist him on them. Now, Mr. Baird, we will creep upon Shed Twenty-three, darting from building to building, taking shelter behind each shed. Are you prepared?"

Left between the containers, Fortney wondered whether sitting would be moving a foot.

"Fortney?" He knew the voice, but dared not move, even when Marais squatted in front of him. "What the devil are you doing jammed between those crates?"

"The inspector and Mr. Baird left me because I sneezed. They went to Shed Twenty-three."

"Since I have more sense than Heurtebise, I've been watching that shed from hiding. I saw Frank go in."

"He heard Ms. Satchel tell me she'd be there! He must know I'd tell the inspector. It's lucky Mr. Baird's along! But I hope the police hurry."

Marais gripped Fortney's arm. "Heurtebise called the police?"

"No. Mr. Baird did."

"Ah." Marais' grip relaxed. "We don't have to expect the police, then. Baird and Frank will put the inspector out of commission."

"Mr. *Baird*?"

"Think. Who was at our table when my mineral water was drugged? Who was at our table the next evening when Ms. Satchel asked you to put the watch in her cabin? And the next day, when she told you to keep it for the trip? And that night at dinner, when you said it wasn't with you? Last night Elena took out the watch after dinner, and again in the Lobelia Lounge, and you had a prowler *after* you were in your suite."

Fortney sat down. "If they put the inspector out of

commission, Frank may tell Mr. Baird I have the watch."

"*You?*"

"Ms. Satchel gave it to me just before she went ashore. Frank came after me, but the inspector must have scared him away."

"You said you didn't have it." Marais' voice was low and terrible.

"The inspector took it. I still have the copy."

Marais' grip on Fortney's arm was like a steel claw. "Does Baird, Frank, *anybody*, know Heurtebise has the real watch?"

"I don't think so. Could you let go of me?"

"Frank still thinks you have it?"

"I think so."

"So Baird would think you have it, then. Then they'll be back for you sooner than I expected!" Marais took a handkerchief from his pocket and spread it against the side of a carton. He handed Fortney a pen. "Print in large letters: *My asthma is worse. I went to get a pill. Fortney.*"

Sniffling, Fortney obeyed.

"Put it on the ground right outside where they can't miss it."

"What if I see them coming?"

"Then you run for your life. Otherwise, come back here."

Spreading the handkerchief on the ground at the shed entrance, Fortney put his billfold on one corner and his coins on another. His heart pounding like a Ping-Pong ball, he raced back to Marais.

They squeezed between two stacks of crates. "Don't even breathe," Marais whispered.

The openings at both ends of the great shed were nearly as large as the end walls, but inside, the huge windowless building was half dark.

Through the shed opening, Fortney saw Baird coming with Frank and another man. Fortney gasped. It was the man he'd seen running from Marais' suite the first night out — the man who'd dropped the watch!

Baird picked up Fortney's handkerchief, muttered something, and showed it to the other men. "I doubt the boy will try to get back through the galley," Baird said. "He'll probably head toward the main passenger ramp — but we can't assume anything. I'll start back toward the galley. You two split up. We have to get that watch before he reaches the ship."

As the three moved from sight, Fortney let out a long, quivering breath.

"Come on," Marais said.

Shed Twenty-three, too, was enormous, dim, full of crates and containers. Marais stalked through it like a panther cat, his voice low. "Inspector?"

"Ms. Satchel?" Fortney followed close, voice shaking.

At last, Marais stopped. "Nothing. They must have dragged him to another shed or . . . worse."

"Shouldn't we try to get the police?"

"I told you, this is undercover." He started for the far door. "Stop sniffling."

"What's that?"

"Where?"

Fortney pointed at a crate.

Marais peered at the lettering on its side. "Just what it says — fen bark."

"What's fen bark?"

"Bark from trees that grow in fens."

"Fens?"

"Moors, swamps, damp places. They use the bark in gardens. Come on."

"Wait." Fortney sniffed, and sniffled. "*Something is cotton in the crate of fen bark!*"

As Fortney tore frantically at the slats, Marais whipped out a pocket knife and pried them loose.

Gagged, trussed wrist and ankle, Darius Heurtebise toppled from the crate in a storm of bark chips. Catching him, Marais lowered him to the floor and began to search his pockets.

"Um . . . why don't we untie him?" Fortney asked.

"Good idea." Rolling Heurtebise facedown, Marais untied his wrists. "Don't move, Inspector." He stripped Heurtebise's jacket off and tossed it to Fortney. "Check the inside pockets." Quickly, he retied the inspector's wrists.

"What are you doing?" Fortney tried to hold back a sneeze.

"Nothing in his coat?"

"Nothing." Fortney put the jacket down carefully, sniffling.

Marais untied the gag. "No shouting, Inspector. You'd only bring Baird and his friends. And don't tell me they took the watch. They still think Fortney has it."

"We'd better find Ms. Satchel," Fortney said.

Marais ignored him. "If I don't get the watch, Inspector, it's back in the crate for you, permanently."

"He'll choke in there!" A sneeze shook Fortney.

"He doesn't matter. Inspector, you're running out of time."

"What do you mean, he doesn't *matter*?" Fortney sneezed again.

"Shut up!" Marais snapped.

"Look for your stupid watch yourself." Kneeling, Fortney began to untie the inspector's ankles. Out of the corner of his eye he saw Marais pick up Heurtebise's jacket. "What kind of secret agent are you?" he muttered.

Before Fortney could move, Marais whipped the jacket over his head. "No kind, I'm afraid. Sorry, Fortney, but you're too much noise and trouble."

As Marais wrestled him to the floor, pinning his arms to his sides, Fortney struggled wildly, wheezing through the wool.

Then a great, confused battle exploded around him, grappling, thuds, grunts. . . . Thrown free, he shook off the jacket, but before he could get his balance,

Michael Baird gripped his arms. Marais was scuffling with Frank and the man who'd run from Marais' suite.

"Those sneezes were like a beacon, Fortney," Baird panted. "Let's have the watch, now."

Frank and the other man had Marais down, his arms behind him.

"The watch." Baird shook Fortney roughly.

Frank was tying Marais' wrists.

He could give them the copy in his pocket, Fortney thought. They might take it for the real watch. But then what would happen to the inspector and Ms. Satchel?

Every moment you create your life, your self.

He glanced down at the inspector. With that glance, they understood each other perfectly.

Heurtebise curled up, then straightened like a broken spring. His feet struck Baird's ankles. With a cry, the purser let go of Fortney.

Fortney ran. *You are choosing to what extent you participate in your own creation. . . .* Instead of sprinting for the exit, he dashed toward a stack of crates that reached almost to the roof of the cavernous shed.

He leaped, he scrambled and lunged from crate to crate. Someone grabbed for his foot, but he kicked backward. With one wild scrabble, he clambered onto the topmost crate, then turned. Baird and Frank were climbing the stack, cautiously, relentlessly.

Fortney pulled the watch from his hip pocket, sending a fall of paper handkerchiefs wafting down on them. Getting to his feet, he held up the watch. "I'll smash it!"

Baird and Frank stopped, shocked faces turned up to him. "Fortney, no!" Baird gasped.

Beyond them, arms bound, Marais struggled to his knees. "You! You had it all the time!"

Blinking away the sweat that half blinded him, Fortney looked down at the purser and steward. "Get off the crates."

They obeyed.

He felt the stack shift slightly. "I want . . . I want you to bring Ms. Satchel here so I can see she's all right. Then you'll let her and the inspector and me go. Once we're out the door, I'll toss the watch in to you."

His heart skidded. Somehow, without even noticing, he had passed the borders of sanity. But how could people who looked so solid be hallucinations?

"Stand against the wall, all of you," Gertrude Satchel commanded. "Kurt, you and your teammates keep them there. Elena and I will lend Fortney a hand."

"Don't let Marais go," Heurtebise said, remarkably authoritative for one lying tied on a floor.

Ms. Satchel looked at the tower of crates. "Unstable. Precarious. Well. I may be missing a few toes and carrying a few years, but I know climbing. Elena, give me a boost. Good. Now, Fortney, don't let the wobbling of the crates distract you. Feel the wobble and then gently counter it — like a dance. Put that watch in your pocket, then brace your feet on my shoulders. Don't be timid. I'm remarkably sturdy."

She was. Sturdy, solid, unmistakably real.

"Excellent. Reach down for my hand, slowly. Splendid." As their feet touched the floor, she beamed. "Fortney Potter, you have the makings of a first-rate climber."

While Elena untied Heurtebise, Marais said coolly, "If someone will free my wrists, and if Fortney will return my watch — I have an appointment."

Fortney glared at him. "You! You pulled the wool over my eyes."

Heurtebise stood. "Over all our eyes, I suspect. But how in the name of delirium did you get that watch, Fortney Potter?"

Ms. Satchel shot back the sleeve of her jacket. "Why, it's a perfect duplicate of mine!"

Fortney leaned against a single, steady crate. "Ms. Satchel, where did *you* get that watch?"

"In my tape recorder. You remember."

"I mean, what are you doing with it *now*?"

"I gave it to Kurt while you were snuffling and sneezing in the bathroom of your suite," Heurtebise said. "You don't think I'd take another person's delicate timepiece into a situation fraught with danger?"

"You took my nephew," Elena pointed out icily.

"Fortunately. Were it not for this boy, I might be something forgotten in the crate of fen bark." He turned to the men surrounded by climbers. "Under whatever powers apply in this case, I place you, Gerard Marais, Michael Baird, Steward Frank, and. . . ."

"And Mr. Arnold," Ms. Satchel prompted.

"Mr. Arnold?" Heurtebise looked at her in astonishment. *"This* is Mr. Arnold, the missing passenger?"

"Not any longer," she said.

There was a thudding of feet as a contingent of police officers burst into the shed.

"Ms. Satchel," Fortney asked, as the officers were sorting those to be arrested from those to be commended, "How did you turn up here?"

"After you left with my watch, Frank deserted me abruptly. I got on a service elevator, but nobody had told me where to get off. I decided I'd have to get ashore and find Shed Twenty-three myself. I was stuck in a crush of disembarking passengers when I heard myself paged. When I got to the Imperial Suite, Kurt said you'd all gone ashore. He told me about Frank and the piton, so we hurried ashore. Kurt's teammates and Elena were outside customs, wondering what had happened to us all. We sent a customs guard for police while we rushed to Shed Twenty-three, and there you were atop the crates, holding off those wretches without a sneeze, a wheeze — "

"Adrenalin." Heurtebise brushed bark from his moustache.

"Nonsense," she said. "What we saw was the essential Fortney Potter."

"Now may I see those two watches?" Heurtebise asked.

Fortney handed him the duplicate.

Heurtebise held it next to the one Ms. Satchel gave him. "Identical. But what does it all mean?"

"Ask him." Fortney nodded toward Marais. "He'll tell you some great stories."

"Is it possible?" Heurtebise murmured. "Is it possible I have met a criminal worthy of the name? Have I found a scoundrel with some flair, some style, some transgression beyond the commonplace?" Taking Marais by the arm, Heurtebise led him briskly toward the waiting police wagon.

CHAPTER EIGHT

AFTER ALL

FORTNEY, ELENA, and Ms. Satchel were driven in a police car to a station where detectives offered them tea and asked them questions.

Later, Heurtebise came in with a tall, ruddy-faced man in tweeds, who seized Fortney's hand. "Quayle, Scotland Yard. You must be Potter, then. I'm honored. And you must be his aunt — my congratulations." To Ms. Satchel, he said, "Inspector Heurtebise tells me you write mystery novels."

"Under the name of Keller," she admitted.

"Keller!" Quayle sat down. "Madam, have you any idea what your books have meant to me? Excitement, terror, pure delight. To encounter you and the most fascinating case of my career in one day!"

"And what is the case all about?" she asked.

"The theft of a formula for a cheap, safe, pollution-free synthetic fuel. It could lessen the demand for oil by 30 percent in ten years — imagine the redistribution of the world's wealth and power! The thief, the man you know as Gerard Marais — "

"You mean he confessed?" Fortney asked.

"They all did," Quayle said.

"I cannot understand why I'd never heard of Marais before," Heurtebise muttered.

"He's rather new, and awfully good," Quayle reassured him, "a master of disguise, a dozen aliases. He was born one Barry Berry."

Fortney set down his cup. "Beriberi?"

"B-a-r-r-y B-e-r-r-y." Quayle spelled it. "Beriberi is a deficiency disease caused by lack of vitamin B_1."

"I know," Fortney said, "but I'll bet everybody in his school called him beriberi."

"Enough to drive an otherwise rotten young man to crime." Heurtebise pronounced the word as if it were displayed in purple neon. "Marais began with the usual thefts — diamonds, star sapphires, Rembrandts, Warhols. One Reuben Shabandar, of a rather unsavory export firm, disposed of the stolen goods for him through contacts with morally untidy collectors the world over. Then Marais, in a master stroke, a pièce de résistance. . . ." Heurtebise paused to quell his relish. ". . . Marais stole the fuel formula, which he then had transferred to a microdot and hidden — "

"In his watch!" Fortney chortled.

Heurtebise eyed him coldly. "*In* an alarm clock."

"An *alarm* clock?"

"One of five thousand Shabandar was shipping abroad."

"Clever." Ms. Satchel took the last Peek Frean biscuit from the tray. "It would be far harder for anyone to relieve him of five thousand than of one."

"Especially if they'd all been set for different times," Elena agreed.

Heurtebise poured the last of the tea into Fortney's cup. "He packed *the* clock with explosives which would detonate at any attempt to open it. Then, in one of Shabandar's cheap export watches, he placed an ultrasonic device, the only way to disarm the clock. This was the watch Marais wore."

"Shabandar arranged for sale of the formula to an international cartel, a group seeking to control the world's energy supplies," Quayle went on. "He sent them the bill of lading for the clocks."

"Wonderfully paranoid precautions," Ms. Satchel marveled. "With the bill of lading, the cartel could claim the clocks, but no one could remove the dot without the watch which Marais had."

"Paranoid people," Heurtebise observed, "make the most cautious criminals. Marais was to accompany the shipment, meet the cartel's representative at Southampton, turn over the watch, and receive half a billion dollars. In very large bills. Then Marais would pay Shabandar a commission for arranging the sale and the transport of the clocks."

"On our ship." Ms. Satchel peered into the empty teapot. "Of course. Airplanes have been hijacked for far less than that formula."

"Can't a ship be hijacked?" Fortney asked.

"It would be a mess," she said. "Planes have only a small crew and stewardesses. Our ship has a crew of hundreds, not to mention the entertainers. Imagine how many hijackers it would take to control *that* lot!"

"To say nothing of thousands of passengers." Elena shuddered. "You should have seen the scene outside our suite last night!"

"And a great ship," Ms. Satchel pointed out, "confined to water, with a top speed less than that of a senile cheetah, is visible for miles and can land only at large ports."

"Exactly," Quayle agreed. "As Shabandar pointed out to Marais, a ship was the safest choice. Shabandar did *not* point out that the purser, a steward, and one of the passengers on this ship were old smuggling partners of his. Also, Marais' four days at sea gave Shabandar time to complete the sale of the export firm and wind up his affairs. You see, with the *entire* half billion the cartel was paying Marais, Shabandar could pay off three accomplices and still come out ahead. He could change his name, move to another country, live in splendor, and forget the squalid business of selling stolen property."

Heurtebise shook the empty teapot. "The first night out, Baird attempted to drug Marais. Then Frank let Arnold into the suite and kept lookout. Arnold was to take Marais' watch and substitute a copy. Then, at Southampton, Baird and Frank would delay Marais on some pretext. Arnold, posing as Marais, would meet the cartel's representative, turn over the watch, and collect half a billion dollars. Shabandar would be close by to collect."

"Fortunately," Quayle chimed in, "everything went wrong. Arnold, unstrung when Ms. Satchel greeted him, was undone when Marais put up a fight. Frank fled at the first sounds of struggle. Arnold, of course, then had to be kept out of sight, in the hold, with rats and the ship's cat. Marais, equally unnerved, hid his watch in Ms. Satchel's recorder."

"Michael Baird must have been stunned when I turned up with it at dinner next night," Ms. Satchel observed. "Ah! I asked Fortney to put it in my cabin, so while he and I were at the film — "

". . . Frank ransacked your cabin," Quayle continued. "Next day, Baird heard you tell Fortney to keep the watch, so after the boy came to the purser's office on his way to the pool, Baird had Frank search the suite."

"But I had the watch by then," Elena said. "And that night, Michael Baird took us to the Caribbean Carnival — "

". . . while Frank searched your suite again," Heurtebise went on. "By last night, when Baird saw you had the watch, he was desperate. While you were in the Lobelia Lounge, Frank set up the rope and piton. After you were asleep, Arnold crept in while Frank stood lookout in the corridor. Today, Baird saw you return the watch to Madame Satchel. He had me lured to the boat deck and Frank attempted to get her ashore. Thanks to Fortney, it all came right."

"I hope you intend to continue in law enforcement, Potter," Quayle said.

"I don't know. I might not have allergies much longer."

Heurtebise put a hand on Fortney's shoulder. "Your allergies, of course, were essential to solving the case. But if you keep that marvelous nose, that uncanny instinct, and dispense with your symptoms, I'd be delighted. I cannot picture the world's master sleuth snuffling and wheezing his way through the annals of crime."

There was a small crowd on the sidewalk as they left the police station. As Fortney passed, onlookers nudged one another:

"That's 'im. Lad's a bloomin' progidy, they say. Can tell you wot's in a room wifout even seein' it."

"Like a physic."

"A wot?"

" 'E means a sidekick. One of them weird types wot gets messages from spirits."

As her taxi arrived, Ms. Satchel hugged Fortney. "You will keep in touch."

He sneezed.

He was not distressed. He had all the time in the world, his world, to set things right.

Fortney Potter, traveler, adventurer, creator of the essential Fortney Potter, hugged Gertrude Satchel, then turned his face toward the Continent and whatever challenge awaited him there.